According To My Father

According To My Father

ANDREW GROF

CITIOFBOOKS, INC.
3736 Eubank NE Suite A1
Albuquerque, NM 87111-3579
www.citiofbooks.com
Hotline: 1 (877) 389-2759
Fax: 1 (505) 930-7244

Ordering Information:
Quantity sales. Special discounts are available on quantity purchases by corporations,associations, and others. For details, contact the publisher at the address above.

Printed in the United States of America.

ISBN-13:   Softcover   978-1-962366-30-4
                eBook   978-1-962366-31-1

Library of Congress Control Number: 2023918446

FOR STEVEN AND CARYL

Viele sind gestorben, Feldhern in alter Zeit,
Und schőne Frauen und Dichter
Und in neuer
Der Männer viel,
Ich aber bin allein.

Many have died, warlords in ancient times,
And beautiful women and poets
And in more recent times Many men,
I, though, am alone.
—Hőlderlin, *Die Titiannen*

MY FATHER SPREAD HIS ARMS.

His wings.

He flew with a minimal effort, soared more than flew, he entered through my bedroom window and exited through the door just beyond the hall where I kept my bicycle, my bicycle vibrated, with his arms by his sides than plunged falcon fashion just above the winding stairs of our building, the fat autumn flies disturbed against the thick windows, the street welcomed him, the air's resistance making him climb and soar once more, beneath him the city lights, the river's dark ribbon, he headed for the hills, darkness suited him, he split the immensity of the skies like a beam that emitted no light.

My dream could not contain him. My father.

He entered then often enough, changing guises, changing shapes, took careful measurements, knew how to appear, linger as well as disappear in a flash, kids' play as far as he was concerned, my dreams holding few surprises for him, he adjusted himself remarkably well to my dreams' circumference before finally destroying it, I kept still, I dared not move, this is inside not outside the dream I'm talking about, he juggled images, an amazing feat that made my heart pound, attached himself to my thoughts that I could no longer control, I shouted out in the middle of the night, pleaded with him, he handed me a mask for my protection, it was with this mask I crossed the boundaries of my dreams, one after the next after the next, I grasped the edge of my bed, thinking

I had waked I descended to my dreams' deeper circles, the deepest then where all was undisturbed, motionless, quiet.

The darkness burned.

My father a shamus.

He solved the city's unspeakable crimes, rapes, murders, apparent suicides, the apparent suicides his favorites, he would not believe that anyone would ever take her own life, lives always taken by others skillful at manipulation time and circumstances, more often than not he proved himself right, serious men gathered in our apartment to beg his assistance, to discuss the progress of his investigations, they whispered among themselves as my father spoke in carefully measured tones, in the dead of night he explored the dark streets, alleys and abandoned lots of the city, mind you, this was just a hobby for him as were any number of other things in life, I begged to be taken along, to witness his amazing skills, his powers of observation and unassailable deductions, very little hidden from his eyes, the power of his intellect, he interviewed the living as well as the dead, the guilty as well as the innocent, he charmed, cajoled and bullied when necessary, exposed all secrets in other words, trading on some and leaving the others buried deep inside. A number of his more famous or notorious cases were written up in the dailies although with no accompanying photograph of even any mention of his name. My father detested images as much as he detested any sort of labels including his own name, he quoted Shakespeare on the subject, 'A rose by any other name,' and made a decisive gesture with his hand that signaled the end of any and all discussion.

My father a magician.

He pulled live animals from within the belly of his cylindrical hat, the animals, disoriented, confused, ran in wild circles about our apartment until they disappeared into the very walls, leaving colorful stains for the maid to brush off. His various card tricks were famous throughout the city as were his various appearing and disappearing acts. 'Now you see him, now you don't,' he said about himself and he either appeared as if out of nowhere or vanished into thin air. He was offered vast sums for the disclosure of this particular trick, which would have come in handy at the uncertain and unfortunate times we lived in. My father a purist at heart. Magic was not to be bartered for and sold like the live poultry and fish exhibited at the various open markets throughout the city. Occasionally he made our maid purchase a number of these, poultry as well as fish, and he subsequently amazed as well as horrified her by changing and exchanging their natural behaviors. The poultry splashed about then dived deep in our immense bathtub and the fish scurried about on the floor, pecking at both real and imaginary bits of food. The maid feared for her life then, feared being changed from something she thought she knew and everyone recognized to something unknown and unrecognizable. My father waved his hand in dismissal of these fears, but this seemed to have the opposite effect of heightening her anxiety at his casting some sort of spell over her. She enlisted the aid of neighbors against my father's magic but these, fearing my father's powers, merely lingered at our door and listened to the imagined noises within. My father greeted them in his hunter's uniform although, as I later found out, he appeared stark naked and bloodied to their eyes.

My father ancient, ageless.

He had lived through countless wars and revolutions, being both victim and perpetrator of terrifying acts of inhumanity against humanity itself. He had raped, maimed and killed with his usual gusto and was in turn raped, maimed and killed himself. On any number of occasions he had stumbled home dragging his own bloody carcass or exhibiting the severed arm, breast or head of one of his victims. He dumped these into my lap and studied my face for any telltale signs of horror and disgust. My father detested weakness in others as much as in himself, and I make sure to stare stoically at the body parts as though they were no more than ordinary objects discarded, found then discarded once more. He laid his hand on top on my head in a kind of blessing that sent shivers through my body.

My father an alchemist in the Late Middle Ages.

He turned common metals into precious stones which he distributed freely among the populace.

As his fame spread so did the danger to his life from the authorities.

Ordinary farmers and woodsmen armed with hoes and axes stood guard by the door of his hut.

My father worked tirelessly throughout the day and night, pausing for brief periods of rest only as the sun rose or was about to vanish below the horizon. He concerned himself neither with the looming dangers nor the welfare of the country folk whose benefactor he had become. His chief pleasure and joy, his main source of satisfaction in the very accomplishment of this peculiar type of magic whose essence he himself barely comprehended. Strange blue and green lights would emanate from his hut in the night and during the day flashes of lightening rivaling the sun's steady glow.

On numerous occasions he was advised to cease and desist by the count's deformed messenger. He took these warnings as mere jests or, worse, misguided insults by the lethargic count. One dawn when he rested and his armed farmers and woodsmen were caught off guard, my father's hut was burned to the ground and its cinders rose high to eventually scatter and fall like black rain across the countryside. The remains of my father's body never identified, they were indistinguishable from the ashes all about. Only a few base metals and precious stones remained intact and these were carted off by the count's horsemen.

My father simply passed from one sleep into the next. The best of all possible deaths judged by all concerned.

It was doubtful he himself was aware of the passage.

My father always slept standing up and never lying down.

He harbored a tremendous fear for the prone position which he equated with death itself.

My father encircled his dreams. Possessed them with an unmerciful grip. In his dreams he brooded on the problem of life and death, separately then fused together. He often held the Angel of Death by the throat or the other way around, they danced the minuet, the waltz, the tango, the samba depending on the time and place of the dream, once a lusty country jig just out of sight of a burnt village. They never conversed as they danced. The Angel because he had no words and my father because he had too many. During the dance each tried to get the better of the other without skipping any beats suggested by the music. They contended as to who would leave and who follow. My father a terrific dancer and the Angel of Death a connoisseur with hardly an equal. In time the dances became contests of strength and will inspiring both awe and fear among the various onlookers who peopled my father's dreams.

My father dreamed with his eyes tightly shut or wide open. It all depended on the dance and the hour, even the minute of the dream. In other words in his dreams my father saw with his eyes tightly shut or failed with them wide open. The dreams often pursued him long after he awoke so my father could not distinguish between what was real and what wasn't. He walked about as if still inside the dream with everything encountered, seen and touched still a part of it. Our maid held him in her arms then both to stop his directionless and often dangerous walk as well as to bring him to his senses.

My father tried to pull the maid into his dreams, to dance with her the way he had danced with the Angel of Death.

Our maid though of sturdy peasant stock with sense and nonsense clearly delineated. Her walking strength more than equaling my father's dreaming one. With her arms tightly wrapped about my father she raised him off the ground where all my father's dreams resided. Without contact with the ground my father quickly regained his sense of reality and on descending gently disengaged himself from the maid's embrace.

Every time my father dreamed, a danger of his dreams spilling out from the contents of his mind and engulfing the apartment, the building, the entire neighborhood.

In my recollection this only happened once though and by then it no longer mattered, my father's dreams no longer distinguishable from the nightmares all around.

Our maid with a great deal of inner but precious little outer beauty.

Her forehead, her eyes, her nose too large for her face, and her lips with a thickness beyond the bound of the merely sensual.

My father often entered her dreams to encounter her inner beauty and attempt to raise, to bring it to the surface.

She moaned at this invasion and expelled my father through her lips and nostrils.

In other words our maid what she was and my father what he.

Any union between the two purely accidental and detrimental to both.

My father set no store by history.

For someone who wandered freely through the ages, history as if nothing to him.

Of the countless stories of the past he told me, he warned me to take none too seriously, history like a maze leading nowhere in the end. History nothing more than the mere passage of time he also warned whose very nature he also questioned. 'We dream, we wake, and then we dream once more,' he told me. 'Facts collide with fiction and fiction with facts,' he said, 'until neither is distinguishable from the other.'

My father often hesitated during his stories.

The words failed to form or on forming simply betrayed him.

My father's unceasing contest with history no less fierce than his ongoing contest with words I often thought.

During the telling of his stories my father stretched himself to nearly limitless dimensions as if to move beyond the boundaries of time itself. I watched as much as I listened, the spectacle of my dimensionless father as fascinating as the stories he told.

Perhaps more.

My father played the piano at a downtown bar.

The customers arrived early and stayed late to miss none of my father's notes, his seamless improvisations.

The melodies all in my father's head before his fingers ever touched the keys of the piano.

He preferred the black keys over the white, at times spending entire nights in hitting only the black keys during his improvisations.

No one ever applauded.

My father quickly moved from one tune to the next to the next, leaving no time for applause, for interruptions.

The owner paid him in booze, in all the liquor my father could imbibe.

My father never drunk during his performances. The effects of his own music more than countered the effects of alcohol.

He began to lean, to sway, to vacillate only after leaving the bar. To periodically stumble.

Our maid had to collect him at odd hours and from different parts of the city.

In major as well as minor emergencies our maid with an unerring sense of purpose and direction. She knew just where to look and what to do.

Called my father by his name which he refused to recognize.

Only after she stopped calling him by name did my father accede to being helped by her.

Peasant fashion our maid carried my father like a bundle on her back. In the dead of night they crisscrossed the city, the maid for some reason preferring a circuitous to a direct route. She sang as she carried, tunes from her childhood and her mother's and grandmother's before. My father rode those tunes as much as her back, lightening the burden of his weight.

Our maid's tunes filled the city.

The city vibrated as she carried my father.

My father plastered posters throughout the entire city.

He performed this labor of love in the middle of the night with nothing but the light of the moon to guide his work.

His posters meant to compete with and even replace the countless political slogans affixed by the authorities.

My father's posters the simplest of affairs. They were neither for nor against anything. They were mere dashes of color surrounding quotes from the great thinkers and writers of the past. The quotes could be interpreted according to the dictates of one's disposition or heart's desire.

No one in authority familiar with the sources of these quotes nor with what they assumed to have been their proper, their definitive interpretation.

They saw a great danger in these innocuous posters, a threat to their personal as well as collective authorities. They invested a great deal of time and effort in deciphering their meanings as well as in tracking down the perpetrator or perpetrators responsible for their postings.

The number of arrests multiplied and dozens if not hundreds of men and women languished in the city's darkest cells.

In his guise as a pastor without a congregation my father visited these unfortunate souls and made them gifts of colorful playing cards to pass the time of day and night.

On their release several of these prisoners became magicians and dazzled their audiences with heretofore unseen card tricks.

Following in my father's footsteps in other words.

The men arrived for the hunt.

Their appearance upset our maid who took them for either hooligans or members of the secret police. My father appeared just in time in his velvet dressing gown to clear up the confusion.

My father hadn't hunted in years. His hunting days behind him he had thought. The men with a difficult time convincing him to join their ranks, in fact to lead them on the hunt.

'No one knows as much about the woods or about killing as you do,' they pleaded.

They called my father by his titled name. A mistake of course, as my father hated all names and labels.

Nevertheless in the end my father agreed to don his hunting uniform if only to keep the men from raising a ruckus in the building and the neighborhood.

They marched down the stairs single file and chanted a hunting song that hadn't been heard in decades.

Although he was not yet old, in fact to my eyes as well as his own my father never would grow old, my father felt like a young man again.

He and the men disappeared for three days and nights as if the earth had swallowed them.

When he returned it was with the carcass of an immense stag with twelve-pointed antlers that he casually threw off his shoulders in the courtyard below.

He gutted and skinned it with his favorite knife, throwing the innards to the starving cats and hanging the skin to dry like a carpet in the late autumn sun.

He carried the carcass up the stairs to our apartment and from his heavy boots dragged blood and mud across the Persian carpet.

'What's to be done,' our maid moaned, 'what's to be done?'

The stench from the carcass gradually filled our apartment and escaped into the streets below.

My father organized a drive for war widows. From which war?

Did it matter?

The last or the one before.

He worked tirelessly in the night from the list of names our maid had compiled for him.

At times my father leaving nothing to chance. He didn't want to miss as single one of these unfortunate women who resided in different parts of the city.

Wearing his dark condolence clothes, throughout the next weeks and months he visited each of them individually.

Some already as old as time itself, others with the blush of youth still on their cheeks.

Some with little or no memory of the husband they had lost or even of the war that had taken them, while others with their eyes still red from the tears they never stopped shedding.

My father formal in introducing himself.

He bowed deep and kissed their offered hands.

The comfort my father brought them came in the form of money, words and other more or less tangible venues.

He left the women, all of them with smiles on their faces. Not a single one with a frown or any word of complaint.

After his initial, his original visits, my father maintained relationships of sorts through sporadic letters and the occasionally renewed physical contacts, although these gradually diminished with the passing years until they altogether ceased.

In the end the grateful war widows and my father's contacts with them just vague memories in my father's head, crowded and eventually eclipsed by other memories of a more lasting nature.

The moon followed my father's journeys. Guided them.

My father disappeared for days, even weeks at a time, headed for unknown destinations, unknown, that is, even to himself. I always wondered how he managed to find his way back home without any maps or compasses to assist him. My father believed in neither maps nor compasses nor any other written or mechanical devices to guide his improbable journeys.

He rested by day and traveled only by night and then only with the moon's unobstructed light as a beacon. In other words the full, the harvest or the hunter's moon. A quarter or even a half moon would not do and neither would a moon covered or even speckled with clouds.

In other words it was questionable not just where but how far he traveled on these instinctive journeys. He may well have covered hundreds if not thousands of miles or just a few yards perhaps, hidden himself in the bushes of the park not far from our building.

On these occasions nothing was said about my father by either the maid or myself. My father as an entity or even a mere topic of conversation ceased to exist for the duration of his journeys. The maid and I both agreed that resurrecting him through words or even images might do untold harm to the actual traveling or resting man.

In other words we left it entirely up to my father to resurrect himself.

When he returned to reenter our lives as well as his own, nothing was asked about nor offered in the way of explanations about his journeys. It was not so much a question of respect or lack of curiosity but simply one of choosing not to meddle with things none of us understood.

During the Renaissance my father one of the first co-called natural scientists. He made painstaking observations of planetary motions and calculated angles, distances which helped him formulate certain correct hypotheses about orbital cycles. He carefully recorded his findings in several notebooks now lost to time.

He conversed informally with the likes of Leonardo and Bacon and exchanged ideas about the nature of light, motion, matter and perhaps even the essence of life itself. It was rumored that Leonardo's drawings of whirlwinds and various other funnels were prompted by and even based on my father's own observations.

On the other hand Leonardo instrumental in arousing my father's interest in inventions, gadgets at once simpler yet more ingenious than Leonardo's own.

In fact my father the first man to fly, and this was centuries before the Montgolfier brothers' experiments and Pilatre de Rozier's actual flight.

Working in the spacious attic of his Florentine house my father treated canvas with certain oils for thinness as well as durability, then cut, stretched, measured and shaped it to suit his purpose. He worked in secret and by night, his daytime job of advising the duke not allowed to interfere with his nighttime endeavors.

In time he heated the air inside his so-called balloon with a burner of his own construction and by treated and twisted ropes attached a spacious and sturdy laundry basket beneath the opening.

It wasn't until the balloon burst through the tiled roof of his house that the Florentines got their first view of a man rising above their city.

Through the narrow streets below they followed the flight above for as long as they could, shouting both praises and curses at this, to them an inexplicable sight.

At one point my father vanished into the clouds, making the Florentines question the reality of what they had witnessed.

My father descended gently over the Arno. He blessed the river as well as the entire city by extending his hands from his sturdy laundry basket.

Shortly after landing on the Ponte Vecchio my father was unceremoniously seized and carried in triumph to the Plaza de la Republica where, to the shouts of the men, women and children of the city, he was gleefully burned at the stake.

Our maid showed my father her wounds.

The various cuts, bruises and colored disfigurations across her naked body, the result of years of living among the brutal peasants of the countryside.

'It will be all right,' my father whispered, 'trust me, everything will be all right.'

His hands steady, his touch firm but gentle.

He inscribed numerous circles on our maid's body to surround every wound both visible and invisible. Our maid squirmed to his touch.

'Only time can erase what time has wrought,' my father whispered.

Our maid shut her eyes and traveled deep inside her wounds encircled by my father.

'What happened yesterday happened yesterday,' my father whispered. 'What happens now happens now.'

Our maid a child, a pubescent girl, a young woman then. Through her wounds she returned to the past only to erase it.

Afterwards she fell into a deep sleep with my father sitting on the edge of her bed and keeping watch.

The past never definitively erased he knew.

One had to keep a careful watch against its repeated returns.

One late autumn afternoon my father gathered all the strays in the neighborhood.

They had to be first chased and trapped but afterwards they followed my father without the least hesitation.

He led them up the stairs into our apartment where they sprawled across the carpets and settled into every corner and on every piece of furniture. Our maid took flight. The sight of all those dogs made her think she was inside someone else's nightmare. She rushed into the street below to dream her own nightmares which at least she had a chance of fighting and surviving.

In the middle of the night my father joined all the dogs in howling at the invisible moon.

Through the open windows their songs, their cries filled the entire city.

My father's periodic departures, his disappearing acts signaled by the music's sudden cessation in our apartment.

Bach, Beethoven, Wagner.

In my father's presence our entire apartment filled with music, all the recordings by the greats of the present and the recent past. Every piece of music prefaced by my father's brief introduction about the composer as well as the conductor resurrecting him.

The walls shook and the windows rattled.

Our maid shut the door to her room to muffle the dangerous sounds.

At the neighbors' repeated complaints various armed men showed up one afternoon to confiscate my father's records.

'You are not a stupid man,' they told him. 'You must realize the havoc you are causing.'

My father's records carefully loaded onto a truck parked below. The armed men some sort of experts in handling the fragile discs.

My father watched from a window with no visible signs of emotion. Records stashed everywhere in the apartment.

No sooner was one batch confiscated than another would appear to take its place.

Our maid, no longer able to stand the music's insistent call, floated just inches beneath the ceiling of our spacious sitting room.

'The dead happier dead but the living happier living,' my father once told me.

Driven by this belief he visited hospitals throughout the city to place himself between the living and the dead, to keep the living from joining the ranks of the dead.

He moved from hospital to hospital, from room to room, from bed to bed with only his words and gestures as weapons.

His preference for patients with incurable diseases and for diseases with difficult Latin names.

Over and over he whispered the names of these diseases into the patients' ears until the patients digested and mastered them. In time the patients' own chants a sort of humming through the various hospital wards.

Afterwards my father exchanged knowing smiles with them, although both the nurses and doctors tried to curtail his visits before altogether banning them.

My father returned exhausted yet exhilarated from these visits. I begged to be taken along.

Begged to share in my father's power over words, over difficult Latin names.

'When the time i right,' he simply smiled and shrugged his shoulders. The time would never be right of course.

I knew that as soon as he had guaranteed it.

With several silent and invisible partners my father opened a bordello, a whorehouse on the edge of the city. It had long been a cherished notion of his that he confided only to his dreams and indirectly to me whenever I heard him speaking out loud during his sleep.

He meant to surpass Parisian and Amsterdam models and have his bordello become not just the talk of the city but of our country and a number of others besides.

No expense would be spared. His silent and invisible partners highly placed businessmen and politicians who placed their entire wealth at my father's disposal.

For his workers he advertised by having young boys distribute clandestine leaflets throughout the city. He sought mature women experienced in the ways of love. None under the age of thirty.

'Mature love for the mature,' was his motto.

'What greater work than the work of love?' he asked our shocked and incredulous maid.

The candidates, most of them stylish, elegant, showed up at all hours of the day and night for their interviews.

My father with his hands full.

He took his job of selection seriously, considering himself not only a connoisseur but the ultimate patron of love.

High as well as low-pitched cries rang out from his bedroom as my father tested each and every applicant and they him.

The evening of the grand opening approached.

Throughout the day my father floated colorful balloons above the city with the letter V boldly emblazoned in red.

V for Vagina.

Of course V, especially in red, also the emblem of one of the clandestine organizations plotting to overthrow the government.

My father knew without giving much thought to it. But how could anyone confuse Vagina with Victory?

On the night of the grand opening the only customers members of the secret police. They arrested my father along with his bevy of beauties for thoughts if not necessarily actions against the established order.

My father and his women driven in open vehicles to the notorious jail in the heart of the city.

My father smiled and waved at the scattered crowds along the route. My father testing the waters.

In his dark cell he experimented with time travel and or with being in several places at once.

Whether he succeeded or not is anybody's guess.

During the guards' visits someone, my father or his exact duplicate, always in his cell. With little training in the occult, the guards simply took the reality as well as identity of their prisoner for granted.

In his dark cell my father hard at work on what he later came to call his 'History of the World.'

With neither paper, pen nor even words at his disposal, my father's 'History of the World' nothing to do with either history or the world.

With something entirely different then.

Under nearly constant observation, by his lengthy bouts of concentration my father convinced the authorities of his danger to the state. A tribunal of colonels interrogated him at length to probe the nature and extent of his conspiracy.

In response my father performed his range of magic acts for them, from his card tricks to animal metamorphoses to his final and astonishing disappearing act.

In the end it was as though my father had never been, certainly not within the walls of the prison.

For fear of appearing ridiculous in the eyes of their superiors, the colonels decided to destroy all my father's records, freeing him in effect not only from the clutches of the state but from his own as well.

My father uninterested in facts.

Of course facts weren't facts in those days but the mere dicta of the authorities. In other words facts in those days were whatever the authorities wanted them to be and they were just the opposite of what my father liked to call his truths of the imagination.

'Be vigilant against facts,' he warned.

Armed with nothing but his imagination my father survived centuries into the past as well as the future. All his difficulties arising in the present and neither before nor after.

In other words time itself just another imaginary truth as far as my father was concerned. It had nothing and everything to do with him.

The authorities amazed by a number of my father's replies to their questions.

My father in the amazing business they decided which may or may not have constituted a conspiracy against the state.

They addressed him by several names, to none of which my father replied. My father not a believer in names, his own least of all.

The authorities presented my father with several alternative genealogical charts in an attempt to fix him in time, to trap him in both the past and the present. My father refused to recognize any of his possible ancestors, dismissing them all with a few derogatory remarks or simple waves of the hand. My father refused to be trapped by either the past or the present.

'What is to be done with you?' his interrogators stared at him.

My father with several ideas, none of which involved the authorities. 'Eppur si muovono,' he told them at one point.

His interrogators ill versed in so-called dead languages. My father had to translate or mistranslate for them. 'And still I move.' he told them

By movement my father with not just the physical but also the mental in mind.

He refrained from enlightening the authorities about this or any other of his remarks.

Except for his evasive, elusive or simply incomprehensible remarks, my father a model prisoner. It was as though he had been born to be captured, interrogated and held against his will. In other words during the entire time of his imprisonment my father exhibited no apparent will of his own.

This confused as well as frightened the authorities. They suspected some sort of trickery or worse. A survival mechanism stronger than their own.

My father now highly sensitive, now immune to physical pain.

During his ingenious tortures my father either cried out at the first sight of needles, wires or pliers or kept stoically, absolutely still. The authorities could not decide whether he was a base coward or a hero of incredible dimensions.

In other words my father kept them guessing. Sense deprivation produced no tangible results.

In his solitary confinement in his dark cell my father as difficult to read as well as to see at times. My father simply blending into the darkness or the darkness into him.

At some point during his imprisonment my father temporarily permanently or permanently temporarily going blind.

In other words he became blind.

This bothered his interrogators more than it did him. My father perfectly capable of groping about in the dark, of identifying objects by touch rather than sight. In other words my father perfectly satisfied recreating the world according to his diminished senses. On the other hand his interrogators fearing my father's blindness as though it were their own.

'The blind better off blind when there is nothing worthwhile to see,' he kidded them.

My father's blindness lasted until his release. His vision returned with his first steps out on the street.

'Once I was lost but now am found,' my father told a perfect stranger, 'blind but now can see.'

The suspicious stranger moved on without bothering to reply.

My father looked terrific in his top hat. Top hats made for him.

In his top hat my father resembled a statesman, a banker, a magician, a clown. He adjusted his hat for the desired effect depending on his mood as well as the circumstances.

He raised his hat and bowed deep to our maid. Our maid with a difficult time telling with whom she was dealing. The statesman, the banker, the magician or the clown.

The sage or the idiot savant.

My father with certain instinctive gestures to reveal his true identity. Our maid desperately in love with my father and he with her.

She scampered to a remote corner or our apartment to avoid contact with him.

Since his imprisonment my father under constant surveillance.

The men assigned to trail him shadowy figures with no distinguishing physical characteristics. In fact my father often confused them with his own shadow or shadows of his shadow.

My father escaped to his ancestral home deep in the countryside whose existence people only surmised without any certainty as to its true location or even its very existence. He traveled by night in one of his many disguises that not even he himself recognized.

His ancestral home, one of many of course, overrun by weeds and clinging vines. It could hardly be distinguished from the forest surrounding it.

He chopped his way by swinging a machete once given him by a slave on a Caribbean sugar plantation. Another time, another place.

Cut and scratched, he entered this home like a dream dreamed long ago.

His own or someone else's.

He gathered and chopped wood to build a fire in the marble fireplace. The smoke rising from the chimney barely distinguishable from the surrounding mist.

He remained at this place a week, a month, a year. In other words free from the clutches of the authorities as well as time itself.

He returned in the dead of night the same as he had left. There was absolutely no change in his outward appearance.

My father with various incarnations and reincarnations.

In other words time with nothing and everything to do with him.

During his centuries' old existence my father a soldier, a beggar, a statesman, a monk, a tyrant and a revolutionary.

A scholar and a lover.

His ancient treatise on love outlasted the Roman Empire before being swallowed by the Dark Ages that followed.

My father a monk during the so-called Dark Ages.

With his vow of silence only certain chants and prayers passed his lips.

He worked in a vineyard in southern France and cultivated his own herb garden. He concocted various medications that he stored in glass jars in his cell. In other words as a monk my father in the business of healing the body as well as the soul.

He made a careful study of the languages of animals and birds, although his vow of silence did not permit him to communicate with them. His precise notations of sounds still exist in the vaulted library of the once monastery now a youth hostel.

While working in the fields he was killed one day by the well aimed arrow of a royal hunter mistaking him for game. The hunter paid the necessary fine to the monastery where my father's skull is still preserved in the locked basement of the now youth hostel.

Indistinguishable from the rest I should add. My father preached and led the Third Crusade. In other words a soldier and a preacher in one. Or a knight errant if you prefer.

His fiery words intoxicating. The strength of his arms and sword second to none.

As a preacher my father touched by divine guidance. As a soldier by cruelties anything but divine.

In other words he was merciless.

My father never arrived at the Holy Land. Bathed in others' blood as well as his own, he was trampled to death by crazed horses not far from Venice.

The wolves with a hard time separating the flesh from the armor.

As a young woman, a Jew, my father survived several Russian pogroms. In his female incarnation my father a creature of great beauty.

Dark eyes and hair and skin smelling of almonds.

The Tsar's soldiers seized her on the run and raped her on horseback. Set her up front and rode both the steed as well as my father.

In his female incarnation my father with wounds that never healed. She birthed several bastards that clung to her as if to life itself.

She made her meager living by singing and begging in the streets or from house to house.

The melodies sinuous, enchanting and as ancient as time itself. In his female incarnation my father with a voice like an angel's. My father a philosopher in ancient Athens.

In other words a teacher as well as corruptor of the youth of the city.

A deformed, a misshapen figure, he nevertheless managed to carry himself with a certain dignity and grace.

His immense head rested uneasily on his broad shoulder.

He moved like a beggar through the narrow streets but planted himself firmly in the middle of the noisy marketplace. This had the effect of making his listeners concentrate to separate my father's words from the pervasive din, his wisdom from the mere cacophony of sounds.

His words have been compared to the sounds of still clearly heard bells ringing in the distance.

In the end my father taking his own life. Drinking a potion especially mixed for him.

Given a choice between life and death, or mere survival and death let's say, my father chose death.

It was the best or the worst decision of his life, the wisest or the most ridiculous.

In India my father sat beneath a banyan tree seeking, waiting for enlightenment.

He got the country right but the tree wrong. No matter.

My father a mere tourist then, swept along by both the physical and the human, in other words the monsoons as well as the immense crowds of the city until he got this notion of enlightenment, this desire to rise above them both.

In the countryside he found his tree.

The wrong tree of course, but there is no need to dwell on that. My father motionless.

For days or weeks, there was no one around to count.

My father without thoughts or thinking he was without them.

He returned home like a smiling ghost, a jovial image of himself.

'Trust me, enlightenment not everything it's cracked up to be,' he told me.

Kidding of course.

He looked for our maid who had fled to the countryside by then. My father an owner of slaves and concubines.

As many as stars in the sky it was rumored.

Every night he chose one or several of his concubines to ease the journey into his dreams. To make it possible in other words.

My father suffering from splitting headaches. His concubines the best remedy.

Near the end of his short but eventful or long but tedious life, it really doesn't matter, he freed all his slaves and concubines.

Except for one.

He chose his favorite concubine to accompany him on his final journey, to make it possible in fact.

Not knowing any better the concubine died willingly in my father's arms.

Both of them dying with smiles on their lips I should add.

My father dabbling in photography when it was just a fledgling art.

In one of his country manors he turned one of the many chambers into a darkroom suitable for his purposes.

'DO NOT DISTURB' he hung a sign on the door. In five different languages.

For the sake of creating or recreating images, in other words of somehow capturing life, my father temporarily gave up drinking, wenching, hunting along with a number of other customary activities of the so-called noble class.

My father nothing if not driven as far as his interests of the moment were concerned.

Compared with today's technologies of instant images my father's labors primitive at best. The basic law the same of course, stretching back to certain optical principles known at least since the age of Aristotle.

My father made generous use of the researches of one Johann Heinrich Schulze concerning silver nitrate darkening upon exposure.

And then advances, certain advances upon those as well.

My father nothing if not inventive once he put his mind to it.

My father carried his cumbersome equipment deep into the woods of his estate. He refused any and all aid from servants much too eager to please.

In the woods he captured images of various two and four-footed creatures which, used to being hunted, had to be caught in flight or on the run and left no more that smudges on my father's plates.

In the still air my father fared better with the trunks, branches and even the leaves of trees.

Among the manor's servants my father thought to have been a magician. Which he was of course but this had nothing to do with his image-making experiments.

Among his so-called friends or other members of the nobility let's just say, my father rumored to have lost his mind.

Which he had of course although not in their facile sense of the words. As a so-called photographer my father after the very essence of things.

In other words through the use of images expecting to move beyond images to the nature, the heart of things.

To hold it in his hands.

Impossible of course which my father soon enough realized, but the impossible never stopped my father, it only spurred him on to ever greater efforts that depleted, exhausted his energies in the end.

Before his final collapse into inactivity or madness or both, my father made one single or singular discovery.

The so-called art of photography driven by nothing more than opposing masses of light and darkness.

Like life itself perhaps.

Vienna my father's favorite city.

This may have been because he had lost his virginity there, lost it any number of times over decades and even centuries.

The woman or women in question no longer a part of his memory or of anyone else's.

She or they must have been something though. One can only guess, attempt to imagine.

In his youth, middle and old age, which stretched over untold years and even centuries, my father endlessly returned to this city to walk its narrow streets as well as broad boulevards, to sit in its elegant restaurants and small cafés, to breathe its stale yet intoxicating air.

Along with his fellow Viennese he listened to the music of Strauss and Mahler, read the rambling writings of Wittgenstein, Freud and Schnitzler, was amazed by the lush and provocative art of Klimt and Schieler at the so- called Viennese Secessionists' Exhibit.

In other words my father truly alive in a city like Vienna.

Along with his fellow Viennese my father welcomed the Anschluss and was one of the enthusiastic crowd greeting the Führer's triumphant motorcade through the city.

My father held up a baby, not his own, someone else's, for one of Hitler's long-distance blessings.

Being practiced in the art, my father knew a good blessing when he saw one.

Or didn't.

It's all a matter of conjecture.

Based on his noble lineage and through his numerous connections my father tried to arrange a meeting with the Führer himself, but Hitler busy with other matters.

My father had to settle for coffee and strudel with one of Hitler's underlings, a man my father intensely disliked for his lack of style, class and worse than ever pedigree.

My father managed to spill hot coffee on the underling's lap, scalding his thighs and crotch.

Unlike the underling my father thought it a great joke, a Spass in other words.

Occasionally my father with an unusual, not to say bizarre sense of humor.

My father arrested within days by the Gestapo and shipped to a remote facility in Germany for political rehabilitation.

For a period my father quite comfortable in the company of gypsies, Jews, communists, homosexuals and the mentally disturbed. He had quite a few meaningful discussions and even conducted clandestine classes about political theory as well as the art of the fugue.

My father a great lover of fugues.

At times you could hardly shut him up about them.

In time my father returned to us a broken yet exhilarated man.

He made me an official present of a yellow star bequeathed him by one of the inmates at the rehabilitation center.

I clearly recall pinning it on one of my dolls that I later burned in the courtyard of our building.

And this is spite of my solemn pledge elicited by my father to guard the star with my life.

Vienna my father's least favorite city.

He hated it with a passion the way he did all other so-called gay, so-called cosmopolitan cities.

All cities in fact.

My father most himself or only comfortable in the countryside. Nothing but silence and masses of light and darkness.

'Better a live dog than a dead lion,' my father told me.

Quoting himself in one of his past incarnations as a Homeric hero.

In other words getting a kick out of recognizing his own words of nearly three thousand years ago.

Then as now my father famous for his sayings, for his quotes.

Some of his sayings open to contradictory interpretations or even beyond the realm of comprehension.

My father a firm believer or disbeliever in the reality principle. In other words he could go either way. He had numerous discussions with Russell and Einstein about this, Russell whom he called Bertie and Einstein whom he called Albert or simply Al. He took long walks in the company of these and other men and women along the California coast. Once in the company of Garbo whom he simply called Gretchen. He loved her silence better than the others' words.

How and when and why he got to America is another story which I never fully credited.

Some of my father's stories beyond belief even to himself.

'What is mind, no matter. What is matter, never mind,' my father quoted himself.

My father no longer a philosopher by then.

As a philosopher my father died roughly twenty-five hundred years ago. My father experimented with his dreams.

In other words observed, studied and followed them to their logical or illogical conclusions.

Were dreams simply the result of wishes imperfectly fulfilled, of rich food inadequately digested, or the underside of life rivaling life itself in its ability of recalling the past as well as foretelling the future?

Against her initial wishes my father enlisted the aid of our maid in the exploration of these voyages as he called them.

'If you can't do this for me, what can your do?' he had asked. 'If not now, when?'

Short of love my father capable of talking our maid into just about anything he desired.

As my father slept and dreamed, our maid sat and kept vigil by his bed. My father the inside and our maid the outside observer. Covering both bases as it were. Our maid chose a hard-backed chair for sitting to keep from dozing off and joining my father inside his dreams.

My father smiled, sweated, moaned and cursed in his dreams. Throughout the night our maid applied cold compresses to his forehead, hoping this would not in any way taint and invalidate the experiment.

My father woke fully rested and with a benevolent smile on his face. In other words greeting the morning the way he nearly always did.

Our maid a wreck.

'I dreamt I was outside and you inside my dreams,' my father told her. 'A refreshing exchange of roles, don't you think?'

Our maid didn't know what to think.

Most of the time she had only a faint understanding of what my father was saying, what he was after.

She shut her eyes and fell into a deep sleep while my father watched from his bed.

While nursing old wounds from the Battle of Lepanto my father mused about sex and love.

Throughout the many centuries of his existence my father understood and embraced the first while pleading ignorance and or confusion about the second. Along with everyone else he felt.

Masses of light and darkness he felt, with sex the light and love the darkness.

Or the other way around perhaps.

This changed or confused him even further only after he had hired our maid shortly before I was born.

Our maid nearly as ancient and as wise or as foolish as he.

In other words my father didn't know what to make of her nor she of him.

Distinctions blurred in each other's company.

My father hated blurred distinctions worse than death itself.

My father operated an old-fashioned carousel in the heart of the city.

This was at the height of the so-called Revolution with grand atrocities and slaughters committed by both sides in the name of justice and freedom. My father cared for neither justice nor freedom, at least as far as concepts or words.

My father hating all concepts and words with a passion equaled only by his passion for sex.

Among other things.

For his stint as a carousel operator my father assumed the role of a bent old man with a long beard like some wandering rabbi of childish joys. A wonder rabbi in other words at a time at war with wonders. The authorities had given my father his operator's license as a kind of joke or simply because they didn't know what to make of him. In other words as a wonder rabbi my father both amused and puzzled the authorities.

My father always with a great love of machinery. The more complex or the more simple the better. It all depended.

He spent his nights oiling and repairing any damage incurred by the carousel's nonstop run the day before. He polished his horses and carriages and even the symmetrical steel poles supporting the entire structure. On cloudless days the sun danced on my father's creatures and poles as well as on the children's faces.

And this in the midst of all the mayhem and killings. One must bear it in mind.

Eventually my father seized, arrested and thrown into prison.

His carousel dismantled and carried off to a secret museum of counterrevolutionary artifacts.

All this a question of time.

Eventually my father paraded through the streets by one or the other victorious sides with a sign hung around his neck.

'WHEN THE CAT'S AWAY THE MICE WILL PLAY.'

Not many understood that sign with the few who thought they did giving it a mistakenly political interpretation.

All this a question of time as well.

My father fascinated by matter.

In other words a dabbler in subatomic physics.

All in his spare time of course and in the secrecy of his country manor chamber that he had once employed as a darkroom for his photographic experiments.

My father a great believer in conversions. From one thing to another to another still.

This applied to himself as well as to his various activities.

In time my father discovered leptons as well as their antiparticles. In other words matter so light as to be weightless for practical purposes. Pure energy in fact.

My father swore me to secrecy. It did not matter to him that he happened upon his findings well before any of the so-called professional and famous physicists. My father's interest purely speculative and personal. My father caring for neither fame nor fortune as the saying goes.

'Who the hell cares anyway?' was the way he put it to me. Particles and antiparticles.

Matter and antimatter.

Everything nothing but pure energy in the end.

Or everything was nothing and nothing everything. My father tried to get me to understand.

Yet how could he make me understand something he barely comprehended himself?

Our maid going out of her way to prepare my father's favorite dishes.

Whether he ate them with gusto or simply stared at and admired them was all the same to her.

So long as she tried her best.

Our maid with untold recipes in her head that connected her with the country of her youth and her mother's, grandmother's and great-great- grandmother's before. Connected her with time in fact. Our maid serving up time in a number of enticing ways for my father's benefit.

Our kitchen perpetually filled with delicious aromas that I associated with both the substantial as well as fleeting nature of time.

Our maid stood and watched as my father ate or simply admired her concoctions.

Certain looks passed between them. No words, just looks.

As a matter of fact my father and our maid rarely talked in any ordinary sense of that word.

Rarely conversed that is.

Either my father lectured our maid or our maid my father, in other words soliloquies colliding with soliloquies. Both our maid and my father of a restless nature that permitted only lecturing without any involved listening. Irresistible forces meeting immovable objects or Aristotle's immovable movers if you prefer.

My father lectured our maid about Aristotle and Freud and our maid my father about chicken farming and the pruning of apple and plum trees. In my father's words the stuffy air of philosophical speculations and in our maid's the bracing of air of tilling the soil.

Here's the thing though.

Neither my father nor our maid truly believing what they were saying.

My father wanting nothing more than to be a simple peasant and our maid nothing more than a respected philosopher.

In other words both swimming against the current of time and circumstance.

Both swimming as well as drowning in each other's company. My father fearing loneliness.

My father seeking nothing so fervently as a solitary existence. Our maid the same.

Our maid fearing loneliness.

Our maid seeking nothing so fervently as a solitary existence.

Neither avoiding what they feared nor getting what they truly wanted.

My father a tour guide to the various historic parts and sights of the city.

The captain of his ship. My father's numerous tour-de-force performances as a tour guide.

Although my father firmly discredited the power and even the very existence of history, he did his best to make it come alive for the credulous tourists who followed him like a pied or pied piper through the various districts of the city.

'Everyone needs something to believe in,' he told me.

Or, 'Ask them what they want and how they want it and let'em have it just that way,' he kidded.

My father looking dashing in his makeshift uniforms which he changed daily to suit the nationalities of his charges.

My father with a gift for languages. In addition to his native Hungarian my father speaking German, French, Swedish, English, Spanish, Italian, Chinese, Japanese as well as several African dialects as though he had been born and raised in different parts of the world.

'Follow me,' he said to his charges in their native tongue and they did not dare hesitate.

My father took them to ancient castles, museums as well as timeless, in other words modern, prisons and whore houses scattered throughout the city.

'And this is the famous Parliament,' he gestured.

Or, 'This is Suranyi's infamous whore house,' he swung wide its doors.

For the most part my father refrained from the use of names. He hated names as much as history itself.

He crossed and crisscrossed the once destroyed now resurrected bridges linking the past to the present or the present to the past. He distributed pieces of bread to his charges to feed the screeching gulls that swooped like stukkas from the sky.

During this period of his life my father subsisted solely from the generosity of his charges.

'Now and again one has to depend on the kindness of strangers,' he explained to me.

He charged nothing for his tours but asked each tourist to tip him according to his worth.

They were confused of course. No one ever truly gauged my father's worth.

Not even close.

In the end the authorities put a stop to my father's so-called guided meanderings through the city. His was proving to be too great a competition to the city's official tours, in fact ridiculing and mocking them.

'Those counterfeit tours,' he called them. Or, 'Lugworms leading lugworms.'

The authorities had him arrested on the charge of defacing the honor of the state.

'What honor, what state?' my father reportedly asked.

They shipped him off to an undisclosed location in the country where they kept him under observation for years.

My father with two different color eyes.

This is down through the decades, the centuries I'm talking about. One dark, one light.

One black, one blue.

No one encountering my father knew which eye to look at, which to trust.

Only our maid trusting or mistrusting both.

In other words only our maid staring him directly in the face. My father stared back.

Our maid's eyes emerald green.

My father with a great love as well as mistrust of all gems, especially emeralds.

At the height of the French Revolution my father stuffed his pockets full to make his getaway and start a new life in England or the Americas.

Only time would tell.

In the end the gems turning out to be fake. Especially the emeralds.

Nevertheless my father stared back.

At the ripe young or ripe old age of thirty of fifty or even a hundred my father fashioned himself a fifty-foot woman.

To even the odds, to better his chances. A female golem if you will.

For materials he used twigs, leaves, grasses, rocks as well as well as a kind of polyurethane foam that had not yet been invented or invented only by him.

He worked tirelessly through countless nights with tender loving care as the saying goes.

Although how can one be sure of something like that?

Strange blue and green lights emanated from his bedroom where the fifty-foot woman took shape and eventually materialized.

During the days as well as the nights now my father withdrew himself from ordinary, that is to say human company.

Our maid pounded on his door then tried to break it down to catch my father and his female golem in unspeakable acts or simply to save him from her clutches.

In her desperation our maid enlisted my aid but even our joint efforts no match for the spells my father was casting.

In the end a fire consumed the golem but left my father and the rest of us unharmed.

A case of spontaneous combustion.

The authorities duly recorded the event but then left their notes behind as though they had neither the desire nor the capacity to pursue their investigations.

All his life my father seeking as well as avoiding emptiness.

In other words my father's solitary existence like a magnet that both attracted as well as repulsed.

Another way of putting it might be the following.

As a renowned mathematician in ancient Greece or Babylon, my father invented zero.

Came upon it as if by accident.

For years, for centuries afterwards the importance of this discovery lost on everyone but my father.

In other words the world playing catch up with my father as it did on countless other occasions.

Zero containing everything and nothing as far as my father was concerned. The beginning as well as the end. Timelessness in fact.

In the middle of the night he pounded on our maid's door. Wanting to show, to share, to make her a gift of his discovery. Zero.

After my father's adventures and her misadventures with the female golem our maid in no mood to open her door.

My father pounded until his fists were raw, swollen. Then he stopped.

He spent the rest of the night in a dreamless sleep in front of our maid's shut door.

My father as if dead to the world.

My father a puppeteer.

This was down through the years, the centuries in fact.

My father fashioned his marionettes to both reflect as well as to mock the times. His shows ostensibly for children but intended for adults.

He invariably set up his theater in the market places of the various capitals of the world, in the midst of poultry, wine and fish merchants as well as hawkers of pots, pans and baskets woven from bamboo and sturdy grasses.

My father liked nothing better than being behind the scenes, than manipulating wooden puppets through strings and wires attached to their limbs.

His joke on the world or on himself perhaps.

His puppets fashioned to resemble real figures from the past as well as the present. My father with an incredible memory for the past as well as an unmatched eye for the present. Time as if come alive in his puppet shows, meaning the past as well as the present.

Which is what tripped him up in the end of course. Or tripped him up any number of times.

His puppets of the present much too real for the authorities' taste, and they charged my father, a mere marionetteer, with lese majesté. An unspeakable crime then as now.

At his public execution my father like a puppet, a marionette. With no wires or strings attached.

When they chopped off his head sawdust spilled like blood.

No one knew what to make of it, least of all my father.

Some people living a lifetime in a minute, others in decades, centuries, even eons.

My father.

Living in his life in a minute as well as decades, centuries, even eons.

My father a great practitioner of the art of condensing as well as expanding. In other words time meant nothing or everything to him.

'Give me life, more life!' he once exclaimed. I forget the occasion.

In other words a minute more or decades or even eons.

My father with his tremendous discoveries or blasé observations.

In other words my father well versed in the art of remembering as well as forgetting.

And this is minutes, decades, centuries, eons I'm talking about. In other words my father could turn on the charm.

To make his life last practically forever or end it on the spot as it were. All up to him.

My father encamped in front of our maid's door. 'Let me call you sweetheart,' he sang in a low voice.

And, 'Somewhere, somehow someone's gonna be kissed.' Our maid fast asleep. Or simply pretending to be.

My father nothing if not tenacious.

He had promised himself to sing as long as it would take.

This was at the time our maid had turned our apartment into a garden, a hothouse. My father making his way to her door as if to a clearing through the jungle.

'Wake up, little Suzie, wake up!' my father sang.

If he was not about to be admitted to her room, and it was obvious he wasn't, my father wanting to enter her dreams.

It was the least he could do and she permit. Our maid's dreams off limits to my father.

Our maid guarding her dreams by other dreams it seemed.

Her dreams within dreams in other words.

The neighbors reported my father's low singing in the middle of the night which sounded like a battle cry or clarion call to their ears.

The authorities arrived promptly and broke down our door.

They hauled off my father who kept up his singing all the way to his cell in the heart of the city.

The secret police went from building to building, apartment to apartment, door to door in search of my father.

In these or those uncertain times someone like my father could not be allowed to roam free.

Like some loose cannon or worse.

The authorities overestimating my father's passions and skills. Or underestimating them.

Take your pick.

My father nowhere to be found.

In other words he could have been anywhere at all, only not where he was sought.

My father with a knack for being at the right place at the right time, or the wrong place at the right time or the right place at the wrong time, or the wrong place at the wrong. Any number of possibilities, although the possibilities not endless of course.

Under persistent interrogation our maid revealed everything and nothing.

In other words she told them what she didn't know and didn't what she did.

My father playing jeopardy with his own life as well as ours.

In other words his life not worth a damn which he always knew or at any rate suspected.

Somehow, and my father himself unclear about this as about so many of the events, the details of his life, but somehow my father wound up in the mountains.

The wrong place at the wrong time in other words. Or the right at the right as far as his escape from the authorities was concerned.

The paths, the cliffs icy, treacherous, the weather bitter cold with a wind chill factor of minus ten centigrade let's just say. And this was night as well as day I'm talking about.

Throughout his long or short life my father many things, in other words any number of things except a mountaineer. The wrong gait, the wrong clothes, the wrong grasps, the wrong attitude.

The highlands negating life as far as my father was concerned. Rightly or wrongly that was his attitude.

And still he climbed, higher and higher or deeper and deeper if that's your preference, for the sake of sheer survival with his very survival constantly tested by the elements.

In other words my father more willing to have his survival tested by the elements than by the authorities. Put his faith in nature's grasp rather than the authorities' clutches.

My father the original adominable or abominable snowman. A large hairy ape-like creature, much talked about but never actually sighted.

When my father finally returned it was in the guise of a tattered soldier, a veteran of wars distant in both time and place.

No one recognized him, not even he himself. Our maid the only exception.

She put her arms around my father and whispered some sort of riddle into his ear.

My father smiled.

He clung to our maid the way he must have clung to the high precipices, the dangerous ledges of the mountains.

My father couldn't carry a tune. Not for the life of him.

In other words my father with a love of but no ear for music. Appreciate it intellectually but without the gift of properly or even halfway pleasingly reproducing it.

This never stopped him of course.

On certain appropriated or inappropriate occasions he sang or moaned or groaned or perhaps even chanted in a low baritone that could easily be mistaken for an animal's prolonged sighs in heat.

For example.

He sang or moaned or groaned or chanted in front of our maid's door and during particularly oppressive interrogation by the authorities.

My father with a way of insinuating himself into his listeners' ears or of throwing them off guard perhaps.

In other words very little or nothing to be done against my father's so- called singing.

Back in the darkest of the so-called Dark Ages, although that's debatable, in his guise as a monk with or without Holy Orders my father the inventor of the Gregorian Chants.

He came upon them quite by accident, his low groans and moans entirely mistaken for something else.

Even by himself.

My father quickly promoted to abbot in which role he excelled until he disappeared into the woods and was never heard of again.

Being the Sultan's favorite, my father appointed to organize the orgy. The smell of sex pervaded the palace.

My father a great judge of female beauty, of what titillated, pleased and ultimately satisfied.

Or not.

In other words the multifarious delights of the flesh. My father the very mullah of sex.

The Sultan impressed on my father the significance, the import of his role.

The Sultan's satisfaction as well as my father's position at court at stake. In other words hope and hopelessness hanging in the balance.

The beauties from different lands, in other words the Sultan's harem, made to parade in front of my father. If you imagine a modern day beauty contest, in other words bathing suit, talent and so-called intelligence competition in one, you get the idea. Only subtract the bathing suit, talent and intelligence parts. Leave only the flesh.

And I'm talking of hundreds, thousands of women. The Sultan a rich man as far as females were concerned.

My father stood on one of the Sultan's settees to deliver a short speech of introduction as well as encouragement.

'Remember,' he told the assembled women, 'remember who you are and what you represent. You are the very embodiment of beauty, grace, and, let's sincerely hope, of joy as well. An honor, let me tell you, an honor to be merely considered, let alone chosen.'

The unwrapped women in rapt attention.

In other words sitting on my father's every word as the expression goes. 'Now let me see what you've got,' my father finished.

No sooner said then done.

The women going into various well practiced twists, turns and gyrations. Humps and bumps and grinds. Think of an old-fashioned burlesque show if it helps.

Only classier.

My father with a hard time deciding. No one said this job was for the faint of heart and mind and gonads.

In the end he wound up with thirteen, the Sultan's suggestion, the Sultan anything but superstitious or simply enamored of a baker's dozen or, given his age and sexual proclivities, knew just what he could and couldn't handle.

The stage set.

The Sultan's spacious bedroom chamber. The cast of characters assembled.

The Sultan, my father and the thirteen unclad beauties.

My father simply an observer, a chronicler of passion's multiple varieties.

The Sultan not known for sharing his personal delights. 'Let the show begin,' the Sultan clapped his hands.

The rest a matter of history as recorded by my father in his blue and gold notebooks.

Now lost to time of course.

The women began with each other while the Sultan observed, studied, my father as well of course, and then eventually, in time and with time, threw himself into the melee, in other words entangling his flesh with those already entangled.

My father's notes hard to decipher, in other words nearly illegible at this point. Nothing but scrawls and squiggly marks.

Be that as it may. Or the facts remain.

The Sultan dead of a heart attack a half or a quarter or even a fraction of the way through the orgy, a sudden and glorious death as everyone later agreed.

The orgy continuing of course.

My father picking up or continuing where the Sultan left off, waste not, want not always his motto, and I'm talking well into the dawn of the next day or even the one after.

No notes remain but a good time had by all one can only assume. My father eventually beheaded of course.

Somewhere, somehow, someone has to pay the fiddler. My father more often than not.

Nevertheless.

My father dying with a glorious smile on his lips. Memorable at any rate.

The wall broke down. What wall?

Does it matter?

My father finally done with becoming. Not being, mind you, just becoming.

My father lost to time in other words. Fed up with it all.

My father facing east or west or north or south, it hardly mattered.

He enlisted on the side of the Allies, crossed the Channel and joined the

R.A.F. which, because of his groundbreaking work concerning the theory of flight, was more than glad to have him.

Something of a coup or feather in its cap.

My father could have just as easily joined the Luftwaffe, but their manners as well as their uniforms less appealing to him.

History or histories, both personal as well as global turning on such insignificant preferences.

My father always with a taste for manners and uniforms.

In his B-52 or Flying Fortress my father looking dashing in his bombardier's uniform.

Leather cap, jacket, khaki pants, black shoes.

Every flier looking the same yet everyone different. Flying over Leipzig, Dresden, Köln.

And bombing them. Berlin then.

My father as if flying into the very heart of darkness. And bombing it.

And then, as I said, something happened. The wall broke down.

What wall?

It doesn't matter.

My father simply tired of becoming, let's just say. Tired of dropping bombs in other words.

My father bailing out. Somewhere over Berlin.

Dropping himself instead of his bombs.

Quite a sight, as you can well imagine, my father's parachute opening at the very last second as it were, a bomb that wasn't a bomb or my father still or no longer my father, he landed more or less gently in the heart of the city, an approximation, landed with a bit of a thud instead of the usual, the feared explosion.

Wandered about a bit.

This is Berlin we're talking about or enemy terrain, although by that time there were neither allies nor enemies, at least as far as my father was concerned, the bombed-out streets, buildings, people, somewhere near Alexanderplatz my father ran into some elephants and lions, escaped and on the run from their bombed out zoo, in other words the animals and my father with quite a bit in common, their mutual recognition practically instantaneous, 'One day I will study only animals,' my father promised himself, 'their language, their habits, their ways of interacting,' it was a promise he fully intended to keep, but back then the animals running one way and my father another, passing like ships in the night as the saying goes, and the bombs still fell of course but no, no longer my father, by then my father simply seeking a way out or in or away, in other words both knowing and not knowing where he was headed, which was my father to a T, 'Fräulein, can you tell me the way to…?' and my father named a place, just any place at all to the first female he encountered, she didn't hesitate a bit, she let my father into the basement of one of the bombed-out buildings where they made passionate love in order to remember or at any rate to keep from forgetting, which only proved to my father that in the end, whatever that end might be, love does conquer all, or, 'Amor vincit omnia,' as he whispered to the Fräulein who was all ears and arms and belly and buttocks and thighs by that time, and so much for a happy ending of sorts, I mean if that can be believed.

Or not.

My father fathered as others childed. It doesn't matter.

At any rate my father great with directions. Always has been.

At different times of his life he parked himself in the middle of the busiest boulevard right in the heart of the city, or my father the original unmoved mover if you will, and he gave directions to whoever would ask, and I'm talking conquering or retreating armies as well as tourists or ordinary locals, I mean sooner or later everyone, but everyone losing his or her way, no one knew this better than my father, 'Which way to the Castle or the Parliament or the barracks?' they would ask, or, 'Which way to the bank, the hotel, the butcher's, the river?' my father most obliging, pointing them all in the right right or right wrong or wrong wrong or wrong right direction, my father like a lighthouse or the Colossus of Rhodes or the Delphic Oracle that replied only in riddles, the main thing was he stood his ground and sent them all on their way, our maid fearing for his life of course, fearing the vengeance to be exacted by those led astray, 'Never mind,' my father shrugged it off, 'in the end one place as good an another,' or, 'In the end they'll all find what they're looking for, or not,' in other words my father simply didn't give a damn or if he did he had a hell of a way of showing it, but so long as he stood his ground like some traffic cop to the confused and forsaken, I mean he wanted nothing more than this out of life, his life or anyone else's, than to be taken for someone who appears to know his way and is unafraid to act on it, at least as far as others were concerned.

In other words my father a magnificent con artist, the best who ever lived or hoped to direct human traffic.

Or my father always shooting from the hip without regard to consequences.

Miss, near miss or bull's eye, they were all the same to him. In a manner of speaking of course.

'A pitcher goes to the well until it breaks,' my father once told me. Meaning?

Who's to say?

But I often pictured the following.

Here my father or a pitcher, and there the world or a well, and the pitcher going so often to the well that it was a miracle the pitcher had lasted as long as it had, and remember, we're talking eons or at any rate centuries, that it hadn't yet broken into a million pieces, in other words broken definitively and beyond repair, nothing but shards in other words with no one to put them together again.

Or, 'When in doubt, make love,' my father also said, in the way of some sort of explanation perhaps although, again, who's to say.

In other words my father not satisfied until he had his heart broken, and not just once, twice or even a hundred or umpteen times until it was finally and definitively broken, broken, that is, without any possibility of repair.

And that took time of course.

And my father with nothing but time on his hands, or time on his side if you will.

Or not.

Hands on hips and head slightly tilted, our maid stood in front of my father.

Not directly but several steps back the way she always had. 'Tell me what's wrong,' she demanded to know.

Our maid no longer young but not yet old, or already old but still young the same as my father, or by then our maid having lived through centuries, eons the same as my father, full of aches and pains from the passage of time, I mean if it wasn't her neck then it was her arms, and if not her arms then her back or her belly, and if not her back or her belly then her hips or knees or feet, I mean at times her entire body nothing but a map of pains, but what concerned her more than anything else was her irregular heart, now slow, now fast, now skipping, now adding extra beats, and, mind you, this at a time well before the now common practice of various corrective surgeries, but, rightly or wrongly, she took my father for some sort of medical maven, I mean had he or had he not cured Charlemagne himself from excruciating headaches that threatened to split the entire empire asunder, 'It's all in your head, Your Majesty,' my father reportedly told the Emperor, but with our maid it was her heart, she could handle the rest of her aches well enough but her erratic heart had her puzzled if not always, not completely worried, so, 'Tell me what's wrong,' she demanded to know, in other words our maid after some rock bottom truth on which she could settle or from which she could view the past, present as well as the future, but here was the thing about truth, at least as far as my father was concerned, my father a firm believer in a time and place for everything, truth no exception, in other words a time and place for truth as well as lies he firmly believed, the trick was to simply know the time and the place as well as to distinguish between truths and lies, my father took a chance, his best guesstimate in other words, 'You're as healthy as a horse,' he told our maid while staring her straight in the eyes, those emeralds he hated to love as well as loved to hate, 'And which horse is that?' our maid asked, kidding or not, and in response my father drew her a picture of a horse, a chestnut mare in full gallop, now, my father anything but an artist but that drawing of that chestnut mare the very picture of health and life to anyone with eyes to see, and our maid took that drawing without further comment and kept and treasured it for the rest of her life.

Or close enough for practical purposes. My father a great impresario.

Down through the ages and among other things or course. Freak shows his specialty.

'Ask 'em what they like and how they like it,' one of his maxims, and he know instinctively that the relatively healthy and well formed liked nothing better than to view the unhealthy and ill formed, because in every healthy and well formed there lurked the unhealthy and ill formed and my father doing nothing more than accommodating, holding up mirrors to nature's hidden natures, for which he was sometimes richly but more often than not just meagerly rewarded, no matter, or, 'It's a living,' as he once put it.

He scoured the countryside for stars for his shows, and this in times of war as well as peace, it simply, it simply didn't matter, or, 'The show must go on,' as he put it, he preferred country to city freaks, city freaks ubiquitous and much too ordinary he felt, think of your conjoined twins, bearded ladies and dwarfs no bigger than their humps for starters and then move on to your one-eyed, one-eared and limbless monsters, in other words my father out to challenge the imagination for reality's, for entertainment's sake, he now drove a covered wagon, an army or just a pickup truck depending on the decade, the century and the part of the country he was scouring, the main thing was his attention to detail, the loving care with which he conducted this search-and-gather undertaking, 'Freaks of the world unite!' he shouted from atop his covered wagon or lorry or pickup truck, 'You have nothing to lose but yourselves!' in other words what was the self compared to stardom and the admiration and or disgust of hundreds of thousands, when my father dreamed, and he nearly always dreamed, he dreamed big of course, the freaks came out in droves, my father played the trombone, both like and unlike Joshua, as he entered each village, town or hamlet, my father considered by many, especially the freaks, as the very embodiment of the Second Coming, 'Come all ye who are burdened and weak of body and mind!' he yelled, he was definitely leading them to the promised land or, at any rate, some approximation of fame as well as fortune, 'He who hesitates is lost!' my father yelled and the freaks understood him as though he were echoing their very thoughts and words, all the rest is history or at any rate footnotes to the same, you can read about it in my father's 'History of the World or My Life' which he always meant to write but never quite got around to, let me just say that at some, at certain phases of his long life the freaks made my father who he was and he who they were, they all cleaned up in other words and lived happily or unhappily ever after, it all depends on what one means by happily or unhappily or even living, but my father with certain sketches, paintings and later even photographs to document these phases of his life, which he would gladly show to anyone who cared to see and even to those who didn't.

My father with a great love of water. Flowing or cascading.
I'll cite just two examples.
As a Jew lined up along the river's bank, my father made the homegrown Nazis the following bet.
That instead of being shot in the back of the head and allowed to simply drop into the river, my father would jump, dive of his own accord, without being shot of course, that was understood, and in spite of the season's swift current and frigid waters cross from point A where they all stood to point B which my father carefully and specifically designated, and if his landing would deviate even a foot or so from the said spot they, the homegrown Nazis, could do with him as they pleased, but if not, they, the homegrown Nazis had to not only reward my father with his life but celebrate him with the title of greatest swimmer or greatest

Jew swimmer, it was all the same to my father whoever crossed the Danube.

The Nazis not just Nazis but men as well and all men love a good or ridiculous bet.

Just the thing to brighten up their dreary labors.

Or at times, not often but at times a funny Jew even better than a dead one.

To make a long story short.

Or, 'My long life made up of nothing but short stories or my short life made up of nothing but long ones,' as my father once put it.

My father dived and swam.

An excellent swimmer by all accounts, an outstanding Jew swimmer, and the currents and freezing water temperatures not withstanding he made it across to the exact spot he had previously designated, his centuries' old training at first as an Egyptian and later as a Greek mathematician helped of course, the waiting Nazis who had crossed by ferry pulled him out, congratulated him then promptly shot him just the same, because a funny dead Jew was still better than a funny live one.

The second example.

In his other life or lives, my father made a careful and exhaustive study of the great waterfalls of the world, not to be mistaken with waterfowls, your various ducks, geese, herons, what have you which also frequently occupied my father's interests, no, waterfalls I'm talking about, like the ones in New Zealand, India, Venezuela and Africa, but of all these my father finally settling on the one along the U.S. and Canadian border, the Niagara I'm talking about, or, 'When you think, think big,' as he expressed it to me, in other words he could hardly resist the challenge where others, who knows how many others have failed, and this was to be my father's first and perhaps only trip to the Americas, whether real or virtual is a matter of pure conjecture, at any rate here or there my father and there or here the Niagara Falls, my father prepared, took his time as he always did with such heart and bone-breaking undertakings, from cured Canadian pine my father fashioned himself a barrel, coated and recoated it with tar on the outside and various hard to come by resins on the in, from his days as a wine merchant in medieval France my father knowing a thing or two about barrels and resins of all types, it goes without saying, and then about mercantiles in medieval France my father knowing a thing or two about barrels and resins of all types, it goes without saying, and then when he was good and ready, but not before, he climbed inside and pulled in and fastened the lid from within, this like so many of my father's other impossible undertakings strictly a solo, a one-man operation, in the final analysis my father trusting no one or no one as much as himself, by rocking to and fro he rolled himself to the appropriate spot and off, off he flew, assisted by gravity but carried by the cascading waters, my father happier than a barrel of monkeys or several moments of delirious happiness let's just say, or, 'What good is life if one can't be deliriously happy every now and again?' as he often put it to me, my father soaring, falling, roaring to a glorious end, what else, with barrel or water meeting water everything split into a million pieces, give or take a few, a few of them recovered of course but that's neither here nor there, in other words not at all germane to the story, my father finally meeting his looked or unlooked for glorious end, for the first or the third or three hundred-third time, no one's counting, but my father finally at one with the elements which was always his dearest wish, his irrepressible desire, I still have a piece of the barrel in the bottom of a drawer somewhere, it was presented to me by the Joint Committee of the Canadian and U.S. Governments for the Preservation of Nature's Untrammeled Power, the ceremony televised of course, which my father would have loved or hated depending on his mood at the time or the time itself from which he would have viewed it.

Apropos everything and nothing.

My father learned the art of love from Sappho.

'What a beautiful woman,' my father said of Sappho when he first met her and she him on the island of Lesbos, I mean when or where else would they have met, or if not then, when and if not there, where, enchantment in the air, it goes without saying, and in spite of certain impossible barriers recognition between the man, that is my father, and the woman, that is Sappho, nearly instantaneous, or, 'You for me and I for you,' as he told her or she him, or, 'All you need is love,' as he sang or moaned or groaned or croaked to her, Sappho accompanied my father's so-called singing on the lyre, and this at a time when lyres were making their first appearance, in other words just coming into their own, and, sure, Sappho's love directed nearly exclusively toward the fairer sex but so was my father's, I mean talk about having things in common, and, needless to say, Sappho more than willing to demonstrate, to teach and my father to observe and learn, I mean theirs the ultimate master and pupil relationship far outshining those between Socrates, Plato and or Aristotle and their numerous disciples, Sappho something of a goddess back then and my father the acolyte supreme, I mean what he learned at her hands and crotch and thighs and feet more than rivaled the hundreds, the thousands of volumes on the art of love through the ages, in fact my father sorely tempted to pen one of his own but without the use of the word love of course, he meant to simply call it, 'What I know,' or, more specifically, 'Sappho and I,' but later on he found neither the time nor, with Sappho gone, the necessary inspiration, so he wrote and rewrote the book hundreds and thousands of times in his head instead, which was perhaps where it belonged, but throughout his long or short life my father never forgot what he learned from Sappho or forgot it only occasionally and always at his peril, in fact on several occasions my father began what he hoped would be lengthy and meaningful conversations about Sappho with our maid, but our maid unwilling or unable to distinguish Sappho from Brillo in a manner of speaking, in other words she suspected my father of being out of his head by then, and too bad, just too bad for both my father and our maid, although how can one say or what can one say about something like that in matters of fact as well as fiction.

My father hid in the bushes in the park not far from our building.

The authorities were looking for him or our maid or me, it hardly mattered, throughout his long or short life my father on the run more often than not or, at any rate, in some sort of hiding, this time it was a combination of both, on the run as well as in hiding, in other words in being on the run my father stayed put or by staying put my father still considered himself to be on the run, the bushes a terrific or more than adequate or simply adequate cover, I mean from there my father could see without being seen, observe without being observed, and if there was anything my father truly enjoyed it was to see and observe without being seen and observed in turn, I mean I can't tell you the number of times I caught him watching, observing our sleeping maid, and that's just one of many examples, and this bush or bushes in the park just about perfect for watching and observing, and I'm not just talking of our maid but all sorts of people in all sorts of activities, walking, talking, pausing, sitting, arguing, even making love in the bush or bushes next to his, I mean if my father wanted a vantage point from which to survey life, and of course he did, he couldn't have chosen better, in fact, if you're looking for some sort of ancient and or Biblical comparison that bush, my father's bush like Moses' very own burning one in which he glimpsed the Divine or the All or, at any rate, the Very Essence of things, I mean Moses neither more nor less satisfied, awed than my father, or, 'I don't know why I haven't thought of this before,' as he later confessed to me, but we can choose neither the time nor the place nor the circumstances, so, let's just say this bush or these bushes quite sufficient for my father's time and place and circumstances, in other words his being on the run as well as staying put at the same time.

The weather, even the seasons changing while my father remained in his bush.

In other words my father like some observer as well as guardian of time.

Dry days and weeks turned to wet ones, hot to cold in fact, leaves fell, piled up and then the snows, my father sticking to his post, keeping his vigil, 'Oh, the things I saw,' he would later tell me, 'the things I can't put into words,' early on in his sojourn our maid discovered my father's bush through sheer chance or instinct, in other words she was almost certain, day and night she left covered dishes of my father's favorite foods by the bush, whether stray dogs or cats or my father consumed them she could never be sure of, still, she hoped for the best, I mean what else under the circumstances, the authorities questioned her at length about my father's whereabouts, she played the deaf and dumb peasant girl to perfection, she even amazed herself, under different circumstances she might well have been a terrific actress, even one of the greats perhaps, but our maid worried about my father, his emotional as well as physical well being, 'How long can he keep this up?' she asked, 'Even Moses eventually descended from his mountain,' in addition to the covered plates of food she began to supply my father with words, certain whispered promises she had no intention of keeping, the bush or bushes stirred, our maid finally getting through to him she felt, 'Let me call you sweetheart,' she finally whispered and there was a moaning, a groaning from the bush, it was just a question of time or of the right words she felt, 'You and I, we're just a couple of tots,' she whispered, at which the bushes opened a crack to reveal my father's light and dark eyes in which our maid saw herself as if in a light and dark mirror, 'Come on then, let's not beat around the bush,' she finally told him at which my father emerged from his place of safety as well as observation post, our maid or my father led the way to our apartment, no one recognized my father as in the bush he had long since lost the ability to recognize himself, but my father followed our maid or our maid my father, led by words, by promises made never to be kept, but our maid did what she had to do and my father what he, and all's well that ends well, even if temporarily, even if for the time being.

The authorities unsure of what to do with my father. Something had to be done of course.

My father a prickly thorn in the side of the establishment. But.

They could not keep him locked up forever and torture only worked while it lasted, in other words my father's subsequent behavior unpredictable to say the least, and killing him would only have created a martyr at a time when martyrs were the last things the authorities needed and wanted, at any rate my father enamored of martyrdom and quite capable of joyfully returning from the dead as he had proved on any number of occasions in the past, 'Jesus of Nazareth with nothing over this bloak,' as one of the more enlightened secret police remarked, exile the same, how could they exile a man already in exile from himself.

So.

In the end.

To keep my father occupied, out of trouble, out of their hair as it were. The authorities set him up with a butcher shop.

'But I know nothing of the slaughter of animals,' my father objected.

To which the authorities, fully aware of my father's activities in the crusades and the various wars and revolutions through the ages, cajolingly but firmly replied, 'The slaughter of animals is no different from the slaughter of men.'

My father skeptical.

To slaughter armed men ready to slaughter you was one thing, but to slaughter defenseless animals, well, my father had his doubts.

The authorities persuasive, though, they weren't authorities for nothing, 'Let's put it this way, comrade,' they addressed my father, in other words of all the choices they presented him the slaughter of animals the least unappealing or the best of all possible bad worlds, and in the end or when he was not busy being an idealist my father something of a realist, they showed him the butcher shop in the heart of town as well as the abattoir on the outskirt, 'Trust us, comrade, soon enough you'll get into the swing of things, the butchering as well as the selling,' they discussed this job as though they were discussing some kind of diplomatic post, and, 'Soon enough you'll get used to the howls, the blood, the smells,' meaning the actual slaughters themselves, 'and in your butcher shop you'll wear a clean apron of course, spic-and-span like the pope himself on his balcony, and all the women, the housewives of the city will come to you for sustenance as well as any other sort of aid, words of advice you may be inspired to dish out along with the cuts of lamb, beef, pork, what have you,' this last part appealed to my father's sense of altruism as well as gallantry, when all was said and done my father liked nothing better than helping women, housewives and or widows in distress, 'Take our hands, comrade,' and my father shook on the deal, neither the best nor the worst he would ever make in his life.

My father carried death about him then.

Our apartment smelled of blood, our walls echoed with the cries of slaughtered animals, but downtown the women lined up for blocks around his butcher shop, the words soon spread, my father as generous with his meats as with his meat, in the end nearly all the women satisfied, some more than others of course but that was only to be expected, the before and after testaments to my father's choice cuts as well as undivided attentions, they exited my father's store with their heads held high, shoulders back and hips provocatively swaying, attendance at the various political gatherings and rallies soon dropped off as more than half the population wanted nothing more than to fondle and be fondled in my father's butcher shop, the authorities soon enough realized their mistake, their political slogans no match for my father's choice merchandise, they slapped a sign on my father's shop, 'Closed for Repairs,' they repaired him right out of business much the way they had established him in it, 'We'll make you a deal, comrade,' they told him, if he would cease and desist his so-called butcher business they would cease and desist shadowing and hounding him, at least long enough for my father to gather, to collect himself, his abattoir on the outskirt of the city shut down with more modern, state-run killing machines taking its place, my father breathed a sigh of relief, although for weeks, for months afterwards the butchering of animals as well as the comforting of women continued in his dreams, in other words, as was so often the case with my father, reality one thing but his dreams something else or his dreams picked up where reality left off, our maid toyed with the idea of entering his dreams in order to put a stop to them but in the end she didn't feel up to the task, in other words my father tough enough to handle in real life without her taking him on in his dreams.

My father set out for the countryside.

He traveled by train and then on foot, any other form of locomotion offensive to his sense of motion, my father's definite preference for moving at a more or less leisurely pace, he liked observing the things he passed or that passed him, 'Beware of speed,' he often warned me, and this referred to all movement including time itself, in other words interior as well as exterior, or, 'A man who doesn't see where he's going is better off staying put,' but the train carried him deep into the countryside, away from the commotion, the entanglements of the city, he walked the rest of the way to his hut in the heart of the forest, for practical purposes the hut abandoned the year round except for late fall, the height of the rutting season when my father visited, he cleared the hut of the various creatures that had taken up residence in his absence, cleaned the fireplace, chopped wood and built tremendous fires that burned day and night, he hunted only what was necessary to sustain him, rabbits and deer in abundance, then he set about his daily visits, his pilgrimages to his sacred tree, a tremendous oak that had weathered the adversities of time for at least as long and as well as my father had, and in proper or improper Greek fashion, and my father liked nothing better than conducting himself in certain long lost classical fashion, my father made love to this tree, copulated with the now smooth hole he had carved centuries ago, that tree like the original female and my father the original male, in other words both sacred and as if untouched by time, my father's cries echoed with those of the rutting stags through the forest, the tree revived to face the challenges of yet another year, my father as well, for the brief period of his stay in the woods my father truly a part of nature then, in other words it would have been impossible to tell where nature ended and my father began or the other way around, he returned to the city both fortified and exhausted, our maid kept a careful eye on him for the days and weeks that followed, she could hardly tell whether my father was now fully himself or someone or thing from another time and place, my father ate and slept little and when he did sleep his visionary dreams collided with everything around, in other words my father's physical return not yet his mental and emotional one, our maid alternated between keeping our apartment burning hot and icy cold to return my father to his senses, when my father finally reappeared as himself he made certain signs and gestures that our maid chose to disregard, 'Just who do you think you are?' she stared at him, 'And who do you think I am?' she made him take a bath in icy water after which she vigorously dried him until his skin burned, in time and with time things returned to normal, or, at any rate, as normal as they could be given the times, the circumstances.

My father looking forward to a time when he would no longer be aware of it.

Of time, that is.

In other words perhaps he had already lived for too long or not yet long enough, he himself could not decide, but time itself the stumbling block he realized as well as the very element that fashioned his being, every thought, gesture, movement of his constituted of nothing but time, and this my father could neither deny nor accept.

In other words he longed to truly explore, outside not inside of time, and what better place to begin as well as end than along our maid's body, he made his wishes known in no uncertain terms, our maid froze, shut her eyes, in other words in my father's eyes she turned into his sacred tree in the forest but certainly not to her own, our maid with no wish to metamorphose into any thing other than what she was, a simple girl, woman from the country who meant to stay inviolate, intact, in her my father up against the human, not the divine, nothing to be gained by his confusing the two, still, he gave it one last shot, my father something of a poet when it seemed advantageous, in other words my father not beyond the use of words when other approaches resulted in failure.

'Sit,' he commanded asked, 'please, sit.'

With her eyes still shut and body stiff our maid nevertheless obliged. And.

Down on his knees, or not, my father began.

'Your eyes like clear, like unfathomable lakes,' and this with her eyes still shut, 'your hair like willows whispering in the wind,' her hair unwashed and stringy just then, 'your lips like rosebuds glistening with dew,' because of the inclement weather our maid's lips chapped just then, 'your skin like snow, your breasts like warm rolls, you veins like rivulets off a mountain,' and so on and so forth, or my father cooking with gas when cooking with gas was called for, in other words he meant to rival the romantic as well as the metaphysical poets of the near and distant past, our maid taken by surprise and or aback, it was hard to say which, 'You ain't heard nothing yet,' my father occasionally added simply as an aside or just to get her to open her eyes and see as well as listen to him, and on and on he went while our maid sat rod straight and blind with her eyes shut, 'Your eyes like jewels, your skin like alabaster,' he said, in other words covering terrain already covered but using different similes this time around, 'If at once you don't succeed, try, try again,' as he once told me, but on the whole, in general I mean, he may as well have been wooing a stick of wood or some plaster of Paris, instead of connecting his words ricocheted, boomeranged and encircled him like a noxious cloud, or, 'If there's one thing you've got to know in life it's when to quit,' as he once told me, which he didn't always of course but did eventually, finally this time around, abandoning his words, his role as a poet, my father stood up as himself, in other words one of his selves other than a poet, 'Here's what we'll do,' he told our maid who by then had opened her eyes, just a bit, 'We'll dance,' my father said, 'let's just dance a bit,' in other words my father perfectly willing to substitute music for words, movement for kneeling and sitting still, he found a record of Argentinean tangos and wound up the ancient phonograph as much as he could, 'Let's tango,' he said and waited for our maid to rise and enter his arms, my father a better than average dancer let me just add at this point, perhaps even terrific as far as some dances were concerned, the tango being one, in other words a great improviser within the rhythmical confines of the music, our maid simply had to surrender and follow his lead, which she did of course even though she had never danced the tango in her life, 'What do you think?' my father asked as he swirled and dipped her, but there was no thinking with the tango, not the way my father danced it, and for a brief spell, in other words for as long as the music lasted, the two of them were freed from the confines of both time and gravity, and I'd like to say that something else, something more happened afterwards, but the tango is just the tango after all and my father my father and our maid our maid, and whatever would or wouldn't happen between the two of them would or wouldn't happen long after, in other words long after that tango was dead and buried in their hearts, but I'm talking of just this one time and one dance now, the rest left up to fate or chance or circumstances the way nearly everything in life nearly always is.

My father not at all uncomfortable under the light. At first, yes, but later, no.

During his many interrogations he eventually came to feel that he was simply giving a performance with his interrogators as his audience, and my father nothing if not a showman, terrific in fact, in other words he could assume roles, personalities to suit nearly every occasion, had his interrogators eating out of his hands before the day, the night, and the next and the next were over.

The circumstances not the best of course.

The stage not a stage but a smoke-filled room with my father under the spotlight in a straight-backed chair.

And his audience partial, not impartial.

In other words partial to my father's eventual demise. 'Tell us what you know,' they said.

And this at the beginning of each performance with no curtains of course, just the light turned on.

Now, my father knew a lot of things of course, more that he could put into words or even remember, but nevertheless he gave it his best shot.

Unfailingly he told his interrogators, his audience not what they wanted but what they never suspected they needed to hear, hadn't my father been dying to write his 'History of the World or of My Life' for decades, for centuries now, and this was as good a time and place as any to test out certain spoken portions of it, in other words my father regarded these interrogations as dry runs for his eventual great work in the near or distant future, in other words even under the most trying circumstances my father perfectly willing to demonstrate the age-old maxim of 'The show must go on.' his face all aglow to boot, 'Are you aware of the upheavals within and without?' he began, and this to men who were the very cause of upheavals just then, but my father meant at all times and places, in other words my father talking about the vicissitudes of time in all times and places, his listeners, his interrogators could hardly believe their ears, 'The universe inherently unstable,' my father continued, 'you, I, everything about us unstable,' my father pulling out all the stops just then, intoxicated as well as intoxicating as far as he was concerned, he was glad for the opportunity to hold forth on his latest thoughts about everything there was, his entire life nothing more than a prolonged waiting for just such opportunities, 'We are born, we live, we die,' he continued, 'and in the end it doesn't make one bit of difference,' my father getting carried away, moving ever deeper into his so-called philosophy although in general, for practical purposes my father the least philosophical person I have ever encountered, the authorities at first curious then amused then simply frustrated, annoyed beyond words, in other words it was high time to move beyond words they felt, they went at my father with their fists then with clubs substituted for fists, in other words my father's so-called philosophy pounded, shattered to bits, not to mention his body of course which could take just so much punishment before shutting down, they hosed him down to revive him, to continue where he and they left off, in this one-sided contest between my father and the authorities it eventually became clear that there could be only losers but no winners, in other words both my father and the authorities with everything to lose and nothing to gain in the end, after several days and nights of this my father released on his own wretched recognizance, in other words unceremoniously dumped on the street in front of our building, an example to himself and to others one can only assume, it was there our maid collected him, gathered up the pieces as it were, 'My sweet, my love,' she whispered during this process, although my father couldn't hear, his hearing badly if not permanently damaged, his eyesight the same, in other words he could neither hear nor see what was going on for quite awhile, which was probably okay by him, by then my father had lived through any number of turbulent centuries, in other words he had heard and seen enough, for the most part my father sick and tired of seeing and hearing the same things over and over and over again, 'Am I nearing the end?' he asked our maid when he was finally able to talk as well as see and listen, 'No, no,' she assured him, 'you're just beginning,' which was her own way of expressing her belief in the cyclical nature of time, in other words endings beginnings and beginnings endings depending on how one looked at them, in other words our maid cut through my father's bullshit philosophy with one of her own, she cradled and rocked him in her arms, and for endings and or beginnings one couldn't ask for better, at least as far as my father was concerned.

My father a terrific entertainer.
One of the greats of all time perhaps. A showman.
And this is down through the ages I'm talking about.
A clown, an acrobat, a dancer, an animal tamer, and this just for starters, a ventriloquist, a mime, a magician, he had them rolling in the aisles in Alexandria, Athens and Rome, not to mention the Winter Garden in New York City on his one and only virtual visit to the city, this shortly after his barrel escapade down the Niagara, my father's gimmick, if that's the right word, was never to leave his audience fully satisfied, to keep them guessing and begging for more, in other words his various exits nearly as exciting as his various entrances, his disappearing as well as appearing acts, through the centuries my father played for kings, potentates, dictators of various persuasions as well as what's referred to as the common, the ordinary folk, the man, the woman in the street in other words, his performances legendary, his names and appearances changed and changing of course to suit his audiences and or himself, the two practically the same to my father's eyes, in other

words my father whatever his audiences or he himself wanted to be, he had costumes for every occasion, to answer every need, in a silver helmet, jumpsuit and boots he had himself shot out of a cannon, and this at the court of the French Sun King no less, my father overshot his mark of course and sailed straight through the royal tent, no matter, the King and the courtiers sufficiently amused, in drab civilian clothes my father performed his inexplicable disappearing act for none other than Lenin himself, Vladimir Ilyich took copious notes and did his best to duplicate the feat on several historic occasions, at Le Havre my father turned himself into a tremendous fish to feed the starving populace with apparently no harm to himself, when Lindbergh landed near Paris is was my father not Lucky Lindy who stepped from the cockpit of the Spirit of St. Louis, and so on and so forth.

A downside to my father's inimitable showmanship or countless incarnations if you will.

After the end of nearly each and every show, and I'm talking hundreds if not thousands, my father with a tough time returning to himself, his original self in other words whatever that may or may not have been at the time, in other words the temptation to stay in whatever character he had created for himself nearly impossible to resist at times, or, 'Of all the difficult things in the world, the toughest is being yourself,' as he once told me, and this in spite of the fact that my father was anything but a philosopher, in other words a man of action rather than deep thought and or beliefs, but now and again he was still capable of certain statements like the one just quoted, without the slightest idea of how he had arrived at it or even of its overall import to the grand scheme of things.

My father strangely invigorated by his performance under the lights. In time of course.

He set out in the middle of the night one moonless night to swim across the river or be swept away by it.

Uncertain himself of its purpose, he told no one of this undertaking.

With goose fat and or axle grease smeared all over his body, he slipped noiselessly into the dark waters, in other words from one darkness into another, with his body the third, if one can count that as a sort of darkness as well.

The river neither cold nor warm, about average for the time of year, its currents neither strong nor weak, about average for the time of year.

My father swam with bold strokes, alternating between keeping now above, now below the water's surface.

In other words he was having a hell of a time.

Or, 'Why hadn't I thought of this before,' as he later put it to me. Now, there are two possible endings to my father's river escapade. One.

In time and with time he finally succeeded in crossing the river, at which time he promptly reentered and re-crossed it, winding up just a few miles below his original point of entry.

Or, two.

In spite of his best efforts the river's force eventually overpowered and carried him downstream past countries with ever changing names and deposited him in one of its deltas by the Black Sea, in other words on of its many lakes and swamps from which my father emerged as something of a new or at any rate different man, the Swamp Creature the locals eventually came to call him, and with this new identity, this new self my father founded a colony of like-minded and appearing creatures who lived strictly near and off the swamps, wanted and had nothing to do with anything outside the swamps, and here my father thrived and achieved a sort of legendary status that entered the myths, the folklores of the lands surrounding the Black Sea and even beyond.

Either or, although my preference for the latter, the make-believe rather than the real.

My father dying to apply his latest theories about the language of birds. For this he had to be up close and personal, in other words live with, confront and communicate with the creatures on a daily, even hourly basis, he filled our apartment with varieties of feathered creatures, some flying but others not, the shrieks, the commotion, the mess invaded our lives from early morning till late at night and beyond, my father firmly believed in round-the-clock operations once he had set his mind on a project.

Our maid made semi-serious preparations to leave our apartment, the city for the countryside, 'If I'm to be driven crazy, it might as well be in the open air than the confines of a stuffy apartment,' she told my father, to which my father's simple but effective reply was, 'If you can create a jungle in this apartment, I can certainly create an aviary,' in his heart of hearts he not only suspected but already knew that it would be impossible for our maid to leave his side, the two of them having already reached some point of no return without as yet an arrival, still, she absented herself for days and nights at a time and on her periodic returns threatened to slaughter some of my father's favorite creatures, his red hawk, his roosters as well as his gray heron, my father made no reply, he simply increased his vigilance over his conversational companions, 'All the birds know what they need to know,' he told me, 'Whereas we know only what we create for our own aggrandizements,' my father meaning to learn from his birds not only the simplest and therefore the most essential truths but also the proper attitudes towards life, death and everything in-between, in other words my father fed up with human attitudes and modes of behavior, my father strutted, squawked and even leapt like his feathered creatures, the only thing he couldn't do was fly of course, but this he considered a difference of relatively minor importance, he held lengthy tête-à-têtes with his blue parrot and gray heron, exchanged hoots and walked through the night with his white owl, foraged for seeds with his Philippine rooster.

'Close,' he confided to me, 'I'm so close.'

Our maid worried for his sanity of course as well as her own, she once confronted him in the middle of the night in a feathered costume to bring him to his senses, my father simply stared and then moved right past her, he could certainly tell the fake from the real, the authorities were eventually contacted, this time by our maid herself even though it nearly broke her heart, they came equipped with nets and traps of various sorts, they locked my father into his bathroom while they went to work, in the end only a few doves were left that finally made their escape through the open windows, my father had to be restrained from leaping after them, in other words my father had lost all ability to know where his birds ended and he began or the other way around, for weeks afterwards he would not exchange a single word with either our maid or me, until finally, one late afternoon he finally addressed her directly, 'I'm hungry. How about a nice chicken soup?' In thanksgiving our maid lit several candles in the nearby chapel, and this in spite of the fact that she didn't have a religious bone in her body, only a number of superstitious ones, but she didn't want to be beholden to anyone or anything, not even to God if it existed.

'There is no final performance,' my father once told me. 'Life nothing but a series of endless rehearsals.'

And having lived as long as he had, untold centuries in fact, there was a better than even chance he knew what he was talking about.

Now and again he tried to engage our maid in conversations along these lines, in other words to impress and perhaps even dazzle her with his so- called acquired wisdom, but having lived nearly as long as he had she saw right through the ruse, 'If you want to get into my panties, why don't you just say so?' she told him, my father threw up his hands in mock despair, all his lofty ideas, his serious words like so much dust in his mouth, in time he tried another tack, a different approach, my father nothing if not resilient, 'How about you and I just rehearse for all we're worth?' he asked, 'And how long would that take?' she looked at him, 'Why, until we get it right of course,' he smiled, our maid burst out laughing of course, my father with a way of both amusing as well as frightening her, 'Rev up you engine,' my father persisted, at which our maid made a low gurgling sound even as she managed to push him away, 'Che serra serra,' she finally told him, the only Italian words she had ever learned in the countryside, and what could my father do or reply to that except, 'A stitch in time saves nine,' which neither our maid nor he himself fully understood, how it applied to the present or any other situation that is.

Still.

During one sleepless night I overheard them talking. Caught them in the act as it were.

Still, it was nothing but words, for once in his life my father fascinated as much by our maid's words as by his own and vice versa, in other words the two of them on a trip of sorts with nothing but words their means of locomotion as well as ultimate destination, in other words both my father and our maid actually listened as well as talked to one another, a lovely humming noise from our maid's room that I can only compare to the buzzing of bees in the distance. Now and again I overheard certain words, phrases, fragments of sentences from which I deduced that my father spoke about what was important to him and our maid about what was important to her, but, still, both of them listening as well as speaking, in other words hearing as well as talking, my father's concerns or topics more of distant and universal matters and our maid's of more immediate and personal ones, in other words my father holding forth about the possible beginning and ending of time, the births and deaths of stars and the ever expanding or shrinking universe, and our maid about the difficulties of life in the city as well as the countryside, about individual births and deaths and all the griefs in between, still, the main thing was that the two of them were actually listening as well as speaking to one another, through nothing but words entering each other's worlds as it were, at the time I thought that up to that point it was the best theater I had attended or at any rate listened to, near the end, in other words towards morning their words became clearer, in other words I was able to hear nearly every word of several exchanges, 'What is it you want from me?' our maid asked at one point, to which, 'What have you got?' my father replied, 'But I'm not one of your grieving widows or fat market women or trashy barmaids,' our maid, to which, 'All the better,' my father, but it really got no further than that, in other words the mental never became the physical, and by dawn my father was back to talking about dark mass and energy and our maid about the diseases of animals and certain unfortunate children, but still, still it was clear to me that something had passed between the two of them that night, in other words what was done would never be undone, and although my father still my father and our maid still our maid, I could never again think of the one without also thinking of the other, that, while not yet physical, in my mind a certain union between the two had already been accomplished, but I was just an impressionable child back then and no sooner did I think one thing than I immediately came up with its opposite, in other words that my father could forever only be my father and our maid our maid and that no kind of union between the two could and would ever materialize, so that by the end of that night of listening I felt I was no more assured than at its start, that in fact nothing of any tremendous importance had happened and passed between the two of them, in other words by dawn I was simply confused and could not make up my mind one way or the other.

'You're not so bad,' our maid told my father. And, 'You're okay,' my father to our maid.

But that's as far as it went.

To celebrate, and there were nearly always as many causes for celebration as for grieving, my father traveled deep into the countryside to rejoice with his gypsy friends.

They were an odd lot nearly constantly on the go, and just this one thing they had in common with my father, another was their 'Why worry' attitude towards life, I mean so long as there was sunshine and music and men, women as well as children, but with word of my father's arrival they headed their covered wagons from diverse parts of the country to my father's estate where they encamped as if awaiting the beginning or the ending of the world.

My father greeted them with open arms, as the saying goes.

Or, 'Mi casa, tu casa,' he told them which they understood immediately without the benefit of translation.

Together they slaughtered pigs, geese, goats, lambs and any other foul as well as two-footed creatures found on my father's estate, from my father's pond they caught fat carp they carried on their shoulders like sacks of grain, the smoke from their cooking soon covered the countryside like gathering clouds before a storm, they feasted for three days and nights before getting down to business, in other words before the music began.

Nothing but fiddles, mind you, with a few bass to reinforce the rhythm, all this in the great hall of my father's spacious country home, my father danced as the gypsies played but in such a fashion that the sweat from the dancer and the musicians appeared to be one and the same, my father kicked up his heels or brought them firmly together on the marble floor, with his open arms my father swirled like a dervish or, 'Like the very devil himself,' as the gypsies put it.

Night turned into day into night, day then night once more and still they were at it, my father and his gypsy friends had broken any number of dishes, mirrors and windows by then, they shattered all sources of images including time itself, gravity itself as if temporarily suspended, my father danced several feet off the floor and the gypsies hovered near the ceiling as they played, because of all the commotion and joyous noise the police finally surrounded the house, they meant to contain it, to keep it from spreading across the land 'like a plague,' their description, but they dared not enter until the music and the dancing had stopped, they feared getting infected themselves, in the end they rounded up all the gypsies and sent them off to inhospitable parts of the country from which they were told never to return, my father of course a different matter, now as on so many other occasions before they simply didn't know what to do with my father, they even solicited his advice, 'Tell us what to do,' they asked, my father held up his arms in mock despair, he finally took pity on his captors and, 'Just do what you must,' he simply told them, which was no help at all of course, it simply confused matters for the already confused officials.

My father pretending to be lame as well as blind.

'And the lame shall walk and the blind see,' he winked at me before assuming this persona.

He first practiced getting about our apartment in this fashion before, much to our maid's dismay, setting out on his 'journey of discovery' across the city.

'But you're both lame and blind,' she objected. 'I'll manage,' he pushed her off.

My father bumped into people as well as object, strangers, acquaintances, friends as well as trees, lamp posts, parked and moving vehicles, open and shut doors, he took a great deal of comfort in recognizing no one and nothing while being recognized by any number of people bumped into, in other words they thought they recognized my father but in the end they could not be sure, on his unusual journey my father broke any number of windows and knocked over any number of careless pedestrians, 'Hey, why don't you watch where you're going,' he admonished them, he turned himself into something of a menace to the city's normal flow of traffic, a one-man army or obstacle to its proper functioning, it was just a question of time before he started bumping into the policemen and soldiers on the street, in the end they wouldn't stand for any nonsense of course, after shoving him now one way, now another they finally carted him off, 'Let's put you where you belong,' they told him at which point my father finally opened his eyes and began to move without any difficulty, the authorities didn't get the joke or the joke all on my father in the end, for disturbing the peace in this ridiculous and unheard of fashion they put him in a cozy cell without windows, here he could bump into the walls and bars all he liked while they kept him under strict observation, they meant to get to the bottom of what made my father tick, was he or was he not some kind of agitator or worse, an agent in the pay of foreign powers, that my father was just being my father never entered into their calculations, such a state of affairs at once too simple and complicated for the authorities to handle.

'Why don't your just confess?' my father was asked.

Now, my father had nothing against confessions per se, sins of his past, present and foreseeable future, and perhaps it was high time he made a clean breast of things, turned his long life into an open book, but if only the authorities could meet him half way and inform him which particular sins of his they were most interested in, in other words my father was confused and his ensuing silence the result of this confusion and nothing more, but once again the authorities could not or would not recognize this simple fact. 'We can hold out a lot longer than you,' they told him, at which my

father simply smiled and shrugged his shoulders.

Finally, to please his interrogators, my father began to manufacture sins he thought appropriate to the occasion, in other words why not give them what they wanted and the way they wanted it, my father not a showman for nothing after all, in other words my father faked his way through any number of bizarre roles and activities for the benefit of his eager listeners, he had himself heading certain underground activities intent on 'liberating the people,' his very words, he went into detail about clandestine meetings and explosives placed in strategic buildings and installations, had the authorities running around in circles in other words while he stayed comfortable in his cozy cell, in the end the authorities didn't know what to believe and what not, were they dealing with a terrorist, a madman or simply a consummate actor, my father relished his performances, he fully expected to be rewarded or executed, whichever came first, in the end it was the latter of course, the simplest solution for everyone concerned, our maid allowed to share my father's last night in his cell, but once again nothing happened between them, nothing physical that is, they simply picked up their convoluted conversation where they had left off, a recording of it now exists in the state archives which no one can make head or tail of, no matter, at dawn my, father led off to be executed, 'Tell them I had a hell of a life,' my father told my maid, she smiled and stroked his face, she knew full well this was virtual and not real reality and was more than willing to play her role, 'Wait for me in the hereafter!' she even yelled out as she waved good bye, 'You bet!' my father yelled back, the execution went off without a hitch, the bullets hitting their mark exactly the way they were supposed to and my father crumpling exactly the way he was supposed to, our maid collected his body and brought it home by taxi, the driver a longtime admirer of hers, in our apartment she gently cared for his body until it was questionably but definitively resurrected, just one of a number of times this had occurred over the long decades and centuries of my father's existence, in other words neither my father nor our maid ready to call it quits just then, to cash in all their chips as it were, 'What's for breakfast?' my father asked, to which, 'Eggs, sausages, onions,' our maid replied, and my father as good as new or old just then, depending on one's notion of time of course.

My father fled across the roof tops.

My father a man forever on the go, on the run to be more precise, if it wasn't one set of authorities chasing him, it was another, and this again is down through the ages I'm talking about, the roof tops his favorite means of escape, Vienna, Paris, Madrid, Rome or those of his so-called native city, it hardly made any difference, or a difference only in the clinging, jumping and balancing acts required, for his audience he had the people on the streets below as well as the authorities attempting to duplicate and follow his progress, in those days, years, centuries my father agile as an acrobat, in other words born for the heights, for crisscrossing the city from above not below, his occasional missteps, slips only added a bit of excitement for those watching from below, the authorities tried to guess his route, follow his changing directions, it would have been simpler to track a sparrow that zigzagged across the skies, down through the ages all the rooftops of all the cities somehow connected, you could encircle or cut through a city in any direction at all if you knew what your were doing, the only problem was where and how to descend, touch the ground and disappear, this was always the weak point in my father's roof top escapades, his judgments on this score nearly always deserted him, he inevitably landed in the midst of the waiting authorities, call it fate or bad luck or simple miscalculation, in the end the authorities of all times and in all places trapped my father without too much difficulty, before imprisoning and or executing him they exhibited him as The Human Marvel or The Original Flying Man, they had him in a large cage where he was made to leap across artificial roof tops, rocks and boulders gathered for the purpose, depending on the time and place his audiences varied in size and appreciation, for example they loved him in Paris but hated him in Madrid and Milan, no rhyme or reason, they just did, but down through the ages the authorities made decent sums from exhibiting my father before finally terminating his act, his life in other words, upon his execution they nearly always discovered they had had the wrong man, that my father was not who he was or the man not my father, still, there is only going forward in time, never back, although in several of his existences my father conducted nearly successful experiments with the latter, no matter, upon his execution a number of cities had my father's body stuffed, mounted and exhibited in museums for the criminally insane to keep the revenues rolling in, although in none of his existences was my father ever a so-called criminal or so-called insane, but, 'That's show biz,' as my father liked to say, and one couldn't argue with the success even if that success was built on out-and-out lies or, at any rate, gross distortions of the truth.

My father trying to make a point.

'How long does it take to get from point A to point B?' he asked Of the authorities, of me, of himself perhaps.

A trick question of course.

My father elaborated, explained without waiting for a response.

'How do we even know that point A and B even exist?' he continued, 'Or that if they exist they are not one and the same or so radically different that we have no right to even mention them in the same sentence? And what of the one traveling from this supposed point A to point B? Is he not already moving while standing still while already in motion? And what of the very motion of time and distances? Are they not intricately linked, in fact one and the same? And if they are, what sort of sense does it make to divide, to consider them separately?'

Once he put his mind to it, my father capable of driving anyone crazy. Himself included, of course.

In fact at times he liked nothing better than to drive others and or himself to the very edge of lunacy where nothing, but absolutely nothing made any sense.

Much to others' and his own amusement and or annoyance my father a great destroyer of common sense.

That is before returning to it full force and embracing it for all he was worth.

Back in Elea was he one of Zeno's most gifted pupils for nothing? Or, 'You don't get bacon from dog meat,' as he once put it to me.

In his role as an artist, which he wasn't of course, my father started decorating or defacing, it all depended on one's point of view, the walls of various buildings around the city.

To our maid's simple question, 'Why? he merely smiled and shrugged his shoulders.

Or, 'Because they're there,' my father replied, Like Petrarch.

Unversed in classical authors our maid simply thought my father mad.

He nevertheless succeeded in enlisting her aid in the purchase and mixing of his paints, 'I'm after earth or putrid colors,' he told her, 'the multitude colors of decaying leaves or flesh.'

Our maid fascinated in spite of herself.

As she often was by my father and his various activities. 'Decay deserves decay,' my father told her.

They set off by night and followed the routes of predetermined maps in my father's head.

They worked their way up from residential buildings, both rundown and elegant, to schools, hospitals, penitentiaries and party headquarters.

'Follow me,' my father said and our maid did just that. They made an odd looking pair.

My father, for some reason, dressed in his hunter's uniform and our maid in her country skirt and blouse, my father carrying the buckets of paint and our maid the various rollers and brushers, their dark shadows now in back, now ahead of them, as if certain of being invisible the two of them not particularly careful about the noise they made, occasionally my father sang and our maid whistled or our maid sang and my father whistled, my father picked the buildings, the sites and they went to work in the dim light or near total darkness, with the colors already mixed the designs simply suggested themselves, all my father and our maid had to do was move their rollers and brushes, they painted abandoned lots, burnt-out forests, dried-up river beds, occasionally skies the colors of putrefying flesh, once started on a wall they hardly stopped until they covered it from side to side and top to bottom, they stepped back, examined and appeared fully satisfied, they smiled and moved on, now and again our maid with a bit of a twinge in her lower back, her age-old sciatica, and my father with the occasional numbness in his right shoulder and arm, the result of a wound sustained in the French or some other revolution, still, they kept going, kept it up, by early dawn much if not most of the city walls covered, the operation a success or, for once in his life, my father succeeding at exactly what he had set out to accomplish, with our maid's aid of course, the city awoke to distorted images of itself, by this time my father and our maid fast asleep in our apartment, the authorities set to work to whitewash the bleak forests and abandoned lots, for awhile it looked as though my father and our maid would get away with their hoax or stunt or artistic statement if you will, but in time some drippings of paint were traced to our building and right up the stairs to our apartment, it seemed neither my father nor our maid exercised sufficient caution in this regard, 'Ah, well, win some, lose some,' my father sighed on being apprehended, but he was the only one taken into custody, at times my father's gallantry unbounded, our maid's role never discovered, brought to light, they moved him from one prison to another across the country where they had him painting the walls a drab gray over and over again, they finally charged him with defacing public property as well as inciting revolutionary ideas, the death sentence immediately carried out in one of the prison courtyards he had just recently painted gray, in spite of this he returned to us the very next day a bit shaken but otherwise remarkably fit, our maid made his favorite soup to celebrate, and for weeks afterwards my father impressed our neighbors by displaying the still open wound on his chest where the bullet that should have killed him had entered, for a nominal fee and to the great delight of everyone he let them not only touch but poke around in the wound, both the men and women feeling as if they were touching the very source of life and death itself.

Kids for free.

My father charged the kids nothing.

My father enamored of unfamiliar familiar places.

Hostels, taverns, guest houses, hotels and motels through the ages.

In other words throughout his long existence my father an inveterate traveler.

In fact he liked nothing better than moving from one village or town or city to the next, a sort of extended pilgrimage without the pilgrim's usual destination, traveling simply for the sake of travel in other words, depending on the time and place he sought whatever accommodations presented themselves at night, entered the rooms, in fact the lives of people who had since moved on, it was my father's way of losing and recovering himself in others' identities through the various personal effects and telltale signs left behind.

My father an expert at reconstructing others' lives. In other words an expert at leaving his own behind.

A brush here, a comb there, although occasionally no more than a single strand of hair on the edge of a basin or sink, sometimes even scents of faint body impressions on beds sufficed, pieces of clothing, scarves, gloves, hats when he could find them, from males or females but certainly females his preference, my father would have liked nothing better than to have reconstructed then run into some nameless female in whatever time or place or inn, in other words to have met up with someone with absolutely no need for introductions, just a man and a woman was always his idea of getting to the bottom of things, a kind of knowledge by instinct or osmosis, the whole thing as if foreordained or happening purely by chance, it was all the same to him, in other words no questions asked, my father forever longing for love on the run as it were, and preferably on some bed where hundreds if not thousands had loved before, in other words this longing on my father's part to be at once everyone and no one, or to be everywhere and nowhere if you prefer, throughout his long existence I'm almost certain he pulled it off any number of times, but, no, not enough to suit his tastes, I'm certain of that as well, in other words this persistent and ineradicable longing in my father to be truly and only himself while at the same time longing, in fact desperate to be someone, anyone other than himself, and what better way to accomplish this than to make love to a woman who was exactly the same, in other words both truly herself as well as someone entirely different, in other words throughout his long life my father always wanting what he could not have or having what he really didn't want, and this just one possible explanation for his endless travels, for his brief or prolonged stays at one tavern, inn, hostel or another, at each place he experimented, registered under different names, without quite understanding them our maid fully aware of these goings-on, 'Off and running,' she would simply comment about my father's frequent disappearances, in her country wisdom she considered him just a man in search of the child within or the other way around, in other words she merely pitied him the way one does a stray dog in search of a non-existent home, on his various returns she welcomed him with open arms and stared deep into his eyes as if to dispel the confusions and frustrations mirrored there, my father quickly recognized and tried to seize his opportunity, with her that is, but sympathy and pity were as far as our maid was willing to go, in other words the last thing she wanted was to become lost in my father's embraces, embroiled in his real or fantasy world, whichever applied at the moment.

My father a close friend of Napoleon's. A confidant.

Perhaps the closest the future emperor ever had.

They had grown up together on the island of Corsica, my father a few years older or younger than the Little General, but even as children the dynamics of their relationship fairly well established, in this particular lifetime my father thoughtful, meditative while Bonaparte fiery, explosive the way he was in all of his, but both enigmatic characters it's fair to say, in his young as well as later life Napoleon would not make a single move before first consulting my father, this applied to women, political intrigues, battles and even the style of boots he wore, not that he always took my father's advice, that would be a gross exaggeration and a total misunderstanding of their relationship, but the need, the urge to consult my father something bordering on the physical and not just the mental, it has been analyzed ad nauseam in countless historical books and essays, suffice it to say that no matter whether or how seriously my father was taken he never deserted Bonaparte's side until the latter had himself crowned emperor, at the ceremony, which my father was forced to attend, he reportedly whispered, 'Enough is enough,' and walked out into the sunshine never to be heard of again, not by Napoleon at any rate, that is not until the once emperor found himself in his last exile on the nearly deserted island of Saint Helena where my father suddenly showed up as an aide to the argumentative British governor, in other words near the end of my father's childhood friend's colorful, dramatic and in some ways tragic life my father gave it one last shot to try to reach him, not to change him in any way mind you, but just to reach him, but dying of cancer as well as toxic dreams Napoleon quite delusional by then, and, 'Who the hell are you?' he reportedly asked my father who merely smiled and shrugged his shoulders at this cutting question, for years afterwards rumors persisted that Napoleon had died whispering my father's name, my father's nickname that is which was known only to the once emperor, but Napoleon may have been whispering something altogether different, like, 'Water', or, 'Light', or, simply, 'Ah, the pain,' it doesn't matter, my father accompanied the remains back to Paris and was present at its entombment beneath the dome of the Invalides where he sang a British drinking song, as he was on the side of the British by then and no longer the French.

My father landed a job at the city morgue.

He was fed up with the living just then, he preferred dealing with the dead, 'The dead possessed of true wisdom,' he explained to our maid, 'in other words a wisdom they don't know they have,' or, 'It's lovely to stare without being stared back,' in other words my father could take his time with the dead the way he never could with the living, throughout his long life he nearly always felt the living slip through his fingers, he bathed and dried each and every body, man, woman and child, occasionally he addressed them, 'And how are you this fine evening?' or, 'So, what do you think of death then?' he pried open their eyes as if in search of his own image, in other words looking for life in death or death in life the way he sometimes did, he admired the sheer beauty as well as the ugliness of the human body at permanent rest, it depended on his mood, 'Don't worry,' he told them, 'you're safe now, you're in my care.' Our maid showed up at odd hours with sandwiches and drinks, my father always taken by surprise at this intrusion of the living on the dead, 'You have no business here,' he stared at our maid, 'none whatever,' 'And you?' our maid stared right back, my father with a grudging admiration for her feistiness, her spirit, he introduced her to his favorite corpses and told her the stories of their lives which he made up as he went along, 'This one a great lover,' he pointed, or, 'This one completely confused, befuddled by life,' he ate his sandwich as he unveiled and explicated, our maid could take only so much of this, in time and with time she found the gap between the living and the dead too much to handle, our maid not nearly as practiced as my father at dealing with the nothingness of existence, she rushed out into the dark streets as if late for some prearranged meeting, and this in the middle of the night mind you, she could no more continue looking at my father than she could the dead.

During his stint at the morgue my father never slept, dreamed perhaps but never slept, the dead doing all his sleeping for him as he did all their dreaming for them, one day he returned bleary eyed to our apartment, he seemed neither alive nor dead then but somewhere in between, usurping his role our maid bathed and dried him the way my father had bathed and dried his corpses, mistrusting his senses my father did not venture out of the apartment for weeks, he locked himself into his room to safeguard the grand secret he had learned or to protect us from its debilitating effects.

To impress our maid my father compiled a list of all his lovers through the centuries and handed it to her like some kind of calling card or resumé.

'Not complete of course,' he explained, 'but they'll do for the time being.'

Some of the names well known of course. Sappho, Helen of Troy, Cleopatra, Heloise. 'I ruined her for Abelard,' my father boasted. Our maid unimpressed.

'Anyone can compile a list,' she remarked.

She came back with a list of her own which included Attila the Hun, Genghis Khan and Alexander the Great.

'Why do you think they called him great?' she smiled. My father crumpled up his list. What else could he do?

'Perhaps there were no other lovers,' my father tried a different approach. 'Perhaps it was just you and I all along.'

Our maid not taken in by such a simple, such an obvious approach.

'Be serious,' she looked at him. 'Don't you think you would have remembered me and I you? Don't you think I would have headed your list and you mine?'

In other words she made light of the whole affair which never was nor could have been, in other words defused the past as well as the present and the probabilities and possibilities they contained.

My father smiled in spite of himself.

'But where does that leave us?' he asked, or, 'Where do we go from here?'

Our maid smiled and shrugged her shoulders mirroring my father's frequent responses.

'Come, come,' she gestured, 'I'll make you your favorite lamb stew and noodles. We're always on safe ground with lamb stew and noodles.'

My father could hardly resist such a heartfelt invitation.

My father no one's fool.

Or throughout his long life my father everyone's fool including his own.

Which never stopped him from doing what he desired or avoiding what he didn't.

'Come, let's stroll through the ages,' he told our maid.

And this just after handing her a bouquet of carnations out of season. For the time and place that is. In other words my father knowing a thing or two about when and where to pick flowers and saving them for the proper occasion.

I'll put it another way.

My father in the remembering as well forgetting business.

In other words throughout his long existence there was nothing my father couldn't remember and nothing he didn't try to forget.

Or, 'Time the essence as well as the enemy of man,' he once told me. I'll put it still another way.

When he said time my father meant both his salvation as well as damnation, just as when he said people he meant both his saviors as well as tormentors.

Our maid understood this without having anyone explaining it to her or handing her flowers out of season.

'But I have so much to tell, to show you.' my father tried for the umpteenth time.

Think of another game,' our maid simply smiled, 'or at least another way of playing the same game.'

My father tried yet another approach.

It was the season of floods, of melting snows and swollen rivers, the river already dangerously high as it cut its way through the city, my father using this simple recurring phenomenon to hark back to ancient, to Biblical times, in other words my father once again pushing things to an extreme to suit his purposes, he tried to dazzle our maid with stories of the Great Flood and of Noah and his ark, 'Desperate times call for desperate measures,' he told her, back then and according to him Noah not just an acquaintance but a close friend of his, in painstaking detail he described the man's drunken ways and disheveled appearance, 'Who do you think got him to start thinking of the big picture, to come up with the very design of an ark and beg, steal, borrow the necessary materials?' to hear him tell it my father the true Noah and Noah himself just his drunken sidekick, 'Let me, just let me tell you what we were up against back then,' my father continued, in his story-telling mode my father practically irresistible, to everyone but our maid that is, through his words and gestures my father with a way of making even the distant past come alive, to contest the present in its very reality, 'no one would trust him, us, Noah with a terrible reputation back then and on top of that he was a poor talker, a terrible salesman, yes, he had his visions of course but in those days nearly everyone with visions, visions a dime a dozen you might say, it was up to me to convince the populace, to put the idea over as it were,' our maid blinked, shook her head but at this point she was not yet ready to interrupt my father, in other words she was waiting for a bit more rope with which my father could hang himself, 'in the end even I couldn't succeed, in those days as in ours the populace a stubborn lot, unwilling to entertain anyone else's facts and or visions other than their own, 'Noah, my friend,' I told the drunken sot, 'let's just do this thing and to hell with everyone else,' with the exception of family members and a few stalwart friends it was just the two of us in the end as I said, and you should have seen that ark, it reminds me now of an immense Viking ship or Chinese bark but, really, there is no comparison, and then Noah had this idea of saving some animals as well, at first I questioned the wisdom of this, you know, I mean ark or no ark there seemed to be just enough room for the people we meant to save, but Noah the visionary not I and in the end visions trump practicality, they nearly always do, so we all piled in, cats, dogs, ocelots, zebras, parakeets as well as people, and not a moment too soon, let me tell you, the flood waters lifted and tossed us around, raised us sky high in fact, and this for days or weeks, I no longer recall, our sense or calculation of time not the same then as it is now, suffice it to say that in the end we all survived, struck land, a few kangaroos and wombats washed overboard perhaps but they weren't what I would call true survivors, no matter, but all I'm saying is that we're facing a flood no less dangerous now than then, so why not put yourself in my care, my dear, trust the man with experience and we'll build our ark, enter it together and in time and with time we'll repopulate the earth, or don't you believe in fresh starts, new beginnings,' and so on and so forth.

In other words my father could lay it on fairly thick whenever the occasion called for it or when he was after something he considered his heart's one and only true desire.

'And all this to get into my panties?' our maid smiled. My father paused to ponder, to reflect.

In other words appearing to give the question some serious thought. "You bet,' he finally smiled back.

In spite of herself our maid couldn't help but admire my father's so-called honesty as well as the inventiveness of this latest attempt.

Her turn now to ponder, to reflect.

'The flood's not bad, I have to admit,' she finally responded. 'A cut above the other approaches. But still no cake or cheese or whatever.'

'Pussy,' my father whispered.

'If you prefer. Still no pussy then.'

All in jest, in good fun of course. Our maid nearly always with a light touch in her various repartees with my father.

We had the usual spring flood.

Except for some damaged wharves the city survived entirely intact.

My father living through the golden age of mountain climbing.

And I'm not just talking of trail climbing with the trails far from steep and the mountains far from challenging.

Petrarch and the rest. No. The real things.

Ascending on hands and feet and using thick ropes, ice axes, steel and boot spikes.

In other words the works.

Mont Blanc we're talking about and a number of other Alpine peaks like the Ortles, Jungfrau, Finsteraarhorn and Mont Petvou.

In other words the works.

Or you name the mountain and my father climbed it. The Wetterhorn in eighteen fifty-four.

Although not a Brit himself my father became a familiar figure of the newly formed Alpine Club of London.

The Brits of course didn't know what to make of him, which suited my father perfectly well.

The outside insider or the inside outsider. Always his preference.

'A cup of tea with milk?' they asked. My father stuck to his potent palinka. 'To put blood in my veins,' he told them.

With Edward Whympers he ascended the Matterhorn.

'What, giving up so soon, Ed' my father was rumored to have remarked before reaching the summit.

And so on and so forth.

In South America he climbed the Chimborago in eighteen eighty and in the Himalays the Nanga Probat in nineteen forty-eight.

A stretch of time of course but time nothing to my father back then or even now.

Everest in fifty-three with Hillary.

To hear him tell it Hillary loved, respected and depended on my father. 'Couldn't have done it without that crazy fool,' Hillary remarked in any

number of interviews.

Under his breath of course.

Or, 'What a guy,' he simply gestured.

Now, in no sense of the word did my father consider himself to be a professional.

In other words neither by nature nor nurture can my father be said to have been a true mountain climber.

No.

He did it simply to prove to himself that he could. Or for the sheer exhilaration of it.

Which was my father to a T.

A key to the man if ever there was one.

At times.

My father totally focused on the undoable as well as inexpressible. In other words my father my father.

Lost to the world as well as to himself at times. He packed up his Trabant.

The worst car made in the Balkans, the worst ever produced perhaps. My father did not let that deter him. Not in the least.

'But where?' our maid asked.

My father made a gesture which our maid interpreted as, 'None of your business,' or, 'I don't even know myself,' or, 'Wherever the road will take me.'

She helped him pack.

The essentials as well as the non, with my father it was always difficult to tell, 'If I only knew where and for how long,' she grumbled, my father paid her no attention, or did or didn't my father knew that it was a time of gas rationing, that cards were being issued only for so-called emergency trips of which my father's could hardly be considered one, to his mind yes, perhaps, but to no one else's, 'Don't forget your long scarf and your woolen hat!' she yelled after him, just in case she figured, his eyes already on the road my father set off with just a wave of his hand, 'Heading for oblivion,' our maid mumbled to herself which was just her way of saying that never but never would she ever forget him, the car started up with an immense sigh or cough or hiccup, it moved in now slow, now quick spasms, it finally disappeared as it made its turn toward the river and beyond.

Our maid knowing a thing or two about my father, about herself.

On the third day of his so-called journey she set out to look for him, she found him parked along the river's edge no more than a mile from our apartment, she approached with great caution and tapped gently on the glass, my father roused from his meditation and or reveries and or dreams, he stared at our maid as if seeing her for the first or the last time, 'You,' he asked, 'here?' she simply nodded and handed him a thermos of hot coffee with rum, my father drank it down in a single gulp, the excess liquid flowing down his chin, his jacket, his pants and down into his hunters boots.

Warming him all over in other words. 'Hits the spot,' my father remarked.

Tossing out some of his essential nonessential things, our maid climbed in beside him.

She asked no questions and offered no comments.

In other words our maid perfectly satisfied in keeping my father silent company on this last leg of his journey.

'Ah, the things I've seen and done,' my father sighed after awhile.

Meaning for real as well as make-believe, on this as well as numerous other journeys.

In the recent as well as the distant past.

'I'm here,' our maid commented, 'right here now.'

'Everything at once too much and not enough,' my father continued. 'You reach for the stars to find nothing but dust or the stars hidden in the dust under your feet.'

'I'm here now,' our maid commented.

You start even as you finish and you're already finished at the start.'

And this from a man who had lived through hundreds, thousands of years.

'I'm here,' our maid said.

'You grow old,' my father continues without looking at her, 'As ancient as the rocks, the mountains, the sun itself perhaps,'

'I'm here.'

'But still young. As young as the mountains, the rocks, the sun itself perhaps.'

And did our maid know that the moon, which my father had had ample time to observe from his immobile Trabant, that the moon was just a chunk of the earth violently cast off by some meteoric collision of the distant past? 'The same as I,' my father added. 'Violently cast off yet still the earth for all that.'

'I'm here,' our maid said.

'Hurtling through space,' my father continued.

Our maid couldn't imagine the things that went through one's head while moving neither forwards nor back but hurtling through space just the same.

'The mind itself boggling the mind,' my father said. 'No escape.' 'I'm here.'

My father talked for another hour of so, to free himself from all the words accumulated on his journey to nowhere.

And all this without looking at our maid even once. Then.

After a period of silence lasting longer than my father's words they both got out and pushed the Trabant back home.

No gas, you see.

But the Trabant as light as a feather, as light or as heavy as my father's words had been.

'And now what do you say to a roll in the hay?' my father regarded our maid before ascending the stairs.

Our maid simply rolled her eyes. My father sold the car at auction.

Something of a classic, a collectors' item by then. Or a sucker born every minute.

Or one man's discard another man's treasure.

'Illusion comes from the Latin,' my father told me, 'Ludere. To play.' My father something of a Latin, Greek and Sanskrit scholar.

Among others.

'Do you understand?' he asked. 'Ludere. To play.'

In other words reality illusion and illusion reality as far as my father was concerned.

Or the play was the thing.

Or all the work and no play would have made my father a dull boy. Which he wasn't.

Never once in his long life.

My father an ambulance driver.

Because at the time, for the moment he could think of nothing better to do with himself, in other words nothing more real and or illusory.

With siren blaring he raced through the city.

Day or night, my father always on call, given his peculiar relationship or non with time that was his preference, the dispatchers respected his promptness as well as his no-nonsense approach to the work, 'He'll be there in no time,' they assured the relative or friend of an injured or dying man, woman or child, and my father always was, in other words he cut corners when he had to, always his preference in life, took chances with his own life but never with others', for the most part he got there just in time or a little before and only sometimes after, in other words too late, my father not only a trained ambulance driver but a fully licensed medic as well, more than capable of handling the sick, the injured as well as the dying, my father nearly always first on the scene and only sometimes last, he patched up wounds, gave oxygen and shot life-saving fluids into barely throbbing veins, jump-started hearts when he had to, and I mean over and over and over again, in other words if my father had had the equivalent of a dime or even a nickel for every time relatives or friends of so-called patients murmured 'God bless you' to him he would have been a rich man, not that he wasn't any number of times throughout his inexhaustible life, in other words rich as well as poor, 'Just doing my job,' my father inevitably responded, in other words whether real or illusory his job at the time was meeting death head on and for the most part defeating it on its home ground, death real of course but what could death do against my father's illusory tactics, my father whispered sweet nothings into his so-called patients' ears, in other words my father whispering into one ear with death into the other, it was a hell of a contest, on the few occasions that he lost my father administered the last rites with all the pomp and seriousness they required, my father not an ordained priest, a monk for nothing, this is the Middle Ages I'm talking about, in other words even in winning death the loser in the end, my father perfectly capable of sending souls directly to heaven, all the relatives and friends convinced of this, 'He or she is in a better place now,' he assured them and they took him at his word, but my father's main concern always with life and the living and not death and the hereafter, needless to say he had insurmountable difficulties with and or doubts about the hereafter, in other words he could take it or leave it but leaving it much more suitable to his personality, 'Let me call you sweetheart,' he whispered to a dying woman and brought her back to life, or, "How about a game of hide-and-seek,' to a child and brought him back to life, our maid not unduly or duly impressed, now and again my father let her ride in the ambulance for company and or audience, our maid stunning in her nurse's uniform, on the occasional false alarms my father parked in some abandoned lot and tried to have his way with her, 'Now why should we waste a perfectly good night and a comfortable ambulance while both of us are willing and able?' he smiled at her, but of course she wasn't, able but not willing that is, 'Some other time perhaps,' she pushed him away and my father drove on, at cruising speed this time until the next call sounded.

For his services my father decorated by the surgeon general, the chief of police as well as the prime minister.

My father examined the medals pinned to his chest, took them off and handed them right back.

'You know what you can do with these,' he smiled at the unsuspecting dignitaries.

For his insolence my father was promptly arrested and shipped to a small town jail where he was eventually shot trying to escape.

Shot in the back like a dog.

In time and with time he returned to us in good health and no more was said of the matter.

Although.

For months afterwards our maid shook with both fear and passion every time she heard the sound of a siren.

'How about I give you the world?' my father said to our maid one fine spring or summer or fall or winter day.

In other words April showers or May flowers or September harvests or December storms.

Take your pick.

Both of them out of doors and appropriately or inappropriately dressed. My father gestured.

'How about I give you the world?' he repeated. And.

'Aren't you getting just a bit ahead of yourself?' our maid smiled. And this after decades, centuries, millennia of both their long lives. Or.

'And just what would I want with the world?' our maid smiled. 'Or do with it?'

In other words the world with as much or as little meaning to our maid as to my father.

Which was quite a lot at times but at others not much, in fact nothing at all.

Or, 'Try again, Charlie,' our maid smiled.

In the midst of the showers or the flowers or the harvests or the storms. My father got down on his knees.

He had done it before of course but never out of doors and never with so much real or illusory sincerity.

'But I have been after you for millennia,' he mumbled, 'or ever since time began.'

Our maid appreciated. It wasn't that she didn't.

In other words our maid not our maid for nothing. Or.

My father not my father for nothing. Still.

"What would I do with the world?' Our maid replied.

For the first or the second or the hundred twenty-second time in his life my father stumped.

Truly, that is.

But not for the last of course.

From down on his knees he inhaled the odors of spring or summer or fall or winter.

Inhaled our maid's scents in other words. And then.

Not knowing what else to do, in other words failing to come up with a viable alternative, he started to sing.

'It's very clear,' my father started, 'our love is here to stay.' And so on and so forth.

Which our maid found amusing.

Not my father's voice of course, which down through the centuries, the millennia drove potentates as well as commoners bonkers, and I'm talking men, women as well as children, no, but the words as well as what there was of a tune.

Which she found amusing. But nothing more.

'Get up off your knees,' she said to my father after awhile.

In other words interrupting my father's so-called song or waiting until just after it was finished.

In other words.

Taking pity on my father and or herself.

'Come,' she said, 'let's go walk in the rain or pick some flowers or help with the harvest or slide on the ice.'

In other words neither accepting nor rejecting my father. "Rise,' she said.

And he did.

And off they went into the sunrise or the sunset, whichever came first. 'But I give you the eternal present,' my father haltingly objected.

'Of course, of course,' our maid smiled. And then.

'Come. Let's just go.'

My father remanded to the state's dreaded psychiatric clinic.

This after brief articles about him in both 'The People's Voice' as well as 'The Truth,' state organs both and both of them more or less mirror images of one another, the articles asserting and in some parts meticulously documenting all my father's contradictory activities, in other words his very existence, because if there was one thing the state couldn't put up with or stomach if you will it was contradictory existences and my father's contradictory existences, in other words his shape or form more visibly annoying than most, in other words as far as the state was concerned A had to either equal or not equal B but not both at the same time, as a mathematician and one-time friend of

Poincaré my father of all people should have understood this perfectly well, which he both did and didn't of course, at any rate the state through fooling around, they truly meant business this time, out to either cure or kill him for good, they hoped, in other words make him into one thing or another but, for God's sake, not something in between.

The so-called doctors went to work. My father absolutely still, unperturbed.

In other words standing, sitting or lying down.

It all depended on the doctor and or the time of day or night. The questions fired off with the effect of shots at close range. Worse.

'Where do you come from?' 'How long have you been alive?' 'What is your business?'

'What do you hope to accomplish?' And, finally, 'Who are you?' Others as well of course.

To all of which my father responded to the best of his ability. Kept silent in other words.

'We'll get to the bottom of this even if it'll kill us,' the doctors mumbled.

Meaning my father of course.

My father made to look at endless photographs of so-called political leaders which he took for art of the highest quality, made to listen to endless recordings of so-called political speeches which he considered poetry of the most instinctive sort.

In other words my father both inspired and not. Accepting as well as resisting inspiration.

In other words the doctors in the dark and my father in the light or the other way around perhaps.

Or.

My father flourished as the doctors stagnated or the other way around perhaps.

But.

By the sixth or the seventh or the eighth week my father had had enough, I mean nothing changing, the walls, the pictures, the photographs, the questions, the faces, everything the same or endlessly repeating itself, and if there was one thing my father couldn't abide it was endless repetition, which was why way back when the Hindus kicked him out of their midst because my father dared to laugh at their notion of endless existences, but at any rate my father had had enough, packed up his meager belongings which included his original clothes on his back as well as some state issued, shirts, pants and underwear, what he didn't wear he put in a Lufthansa bag which had always been his airline of choice even though my father never flew, not once in his life, and 'It's been real, boys,' he waved, or simply, 'Swell,' and with that very wave of his hand he transformed himself into a condor or golden eagle or, more than likely, just a sparrow hawk, my father not a magician at the court of Charlemagne and other places and time for nothing, in other words it was high time to really show those doctors a thing or two and high tail or feather it out of there, after breaking through the high window my father circled for a spell then flew in a straight line to our building and through the open window of our kitchen, the journey of questionable duration, in other words once again my father's sense of time not the same as everyone else's, our maid didn't recognize him at first, she had never seen a sparrow hawk up close, only at a distance, but then to prove that seeing was believing or believing seeing my father quickly transformed himself into himself once more, in other words before her very eyes, and, 'My God, is that you?' our maid exclaimed or sighed or simply smiled, and my father just flapped his no longer existing wings, in other words just raised his arms, and to further prove the veracity or our maid's vision and or of his own existence he simply asked, 'Is that lamb stew I smell?'

My father followed a woman down the street. A slight drizzle, early September, say.

In other words the gentlest of rains. Still.

But he followed her because she reminded him of someone other than herself or only of herself perhaps, in other words the total, the perfect stranger, and what was she doing out in this rain, no matter how gentle, and where was she going, without an umbrella needless to say, and my father liked the way her clothes stuck to her body, I mean ever so slightly, and the set of her shoulders and the color of her hair which was still light in spite of being somewhat wet, and in time and with time my father caught up, walking neither too fast nor too slow as was his wont, in other words my father leaving it more or less although not entirely up to fate, or, if he was meant to catch up, he thought, then sooner or later he would, and he did, and, something wistful about this woman, he also thought, and this from just seeing her from the back and at a distance and not yet from the front and up close, 'Hold, hold on,' my father may have even said, to her or, more than likely, only to himself, the woman neither terribly surprised nor upset by my father's sudden appearance, in other words she may well have been used to this sort of thing, hard to say, a beauty of the first order my father later recalled, although according to him all women beauties if not of the first then of the second or, at the very least, the third order, and just when he was on the verge of saying to this beauty of the first order, 'Come, come away with me,' she stared at him directly in the face, and, please, don't forget the drizzle, the gentle rain, and we may as well mention the color of her eyes, they were sky or sea or corn flower blue, but at any rate she said or asked, 'Yes?' and even though yes was my father's favorite word in the language, in all languages as a matter of fact, the very way this woman, this beauty of the first order had said or asked it had the undesired effect of simply putting my father in his place, whatever that place was or may have been at the time, but not, I repeat, not the place my father wanted, this much clear, my father then with just one, just a single choice left, short of walking away that is, so, he took it, 'How about an espresso?' he asked, and given the time, the place, the circumstances, again, the gentle rain, the woman, this beauty of the first order didn't refuse, so long, I repeat, so long as it was clearly understood that an espresso would be the beginning as well as the end, at any rate, 'An espresso would be nice,' she said, and she took his arm or he hers, this particular detail less than essential, and off, off they went to the nearest bar or confectionary, whichever came first, and there, at a window table so they could still watch while no longer being in the rain, they exchanged the stories of their lives, which was something of course but not everything, in other words not all my father wanted, but he simply had to let go, make do as on other such numerous occasions, in other words leave the woman to her life while retaining his, and this simply broke my father's heart exactly the way it had on other such numerous occasions, in other words my father's terribly long and in some ways adventurous life can be traced by markers of broken hearts if you will, I'll put it another way, regardless of the time and place when you think of my father you must think of a man with a broken heart, I mean that's certainly one way, at any rate this woman and my father parted as friends, more or less, but they made no plans to ever see each other again, that was understood, and my father went his way and the woman hers, the rain had stopped or abated by then, in other words the slight drizzle slighter now than it had been before, so that was all right, but the main thing was the woman went her way and my father his, there was no way of getting around this particular fact of life, and this broke by father's heart, of course it did.

My father dead of a broken heart.

One of his many deaths of course but his broken-hearted ones the worst by far, his chest as if caved in as he was laid out, his unfulfilled desires nothing but a stiff mask on his face, his death mask as it were, 'Rest in peace,' our maid mumbled but she knew he wouldn't, not after a death like this, all of us as if late arrivals by the time he was laid out, too late to intervene, to alter this particular finality of this particular life, meaning this death of his, all the mourners filed past, there weren't that many given the importance, the significance of my father's life, 'Here today, gone tomorrow,' the rabbi intoned, a rabbi because no one else was available, but, 'Here today, gone today,' he should have said, perhaps meant to, at any rate words useless in the end, perhaps in the beginning and middle as well but certainly at the end.

Although.

'My wounded heart,' he whispered to me just before he passed on as they say, in other words a dying man's confession, or nearing death, this particular death, my father taking me into his confidence, 'Where am I?' he also whispered, although there was nothing particularly noteworthy in this as through his terribly long life my father had existed in more places than he could clearly recall, but, 'To live past one's life is a perilous thing,' he also whispered, of which I could make no head or tail at the time, no matter, but, 'Life a work of fiction,' he also whispered, and this was where it got a bit more involved or interesting or complicated, but, 'Life is a work of fiction,,' he whispered, 'with names, characters, places and incidents constantly changing to protect the guilty,' yes, he said guilty not innocent, and also, 'Any resemblance to actual events and or persons strictly intentional,' and that's when I walked out, I mean I had had enough, and by the time I returned my father already dead.

Of a broken heart as I said. But.

And one must attach no Biblical importance to this, but after three days my father rose again from the dead, I mean he had always managed it before, after all his other deaths I mean, but this time it was precisely after three days, on the nose I mean, and he simply walked out of our maid's room where she had hidden his body as if for safekeeping, and 'Where is the sun?' he asked, 'The sun should be out by now,' but as it was a cloudy day there was no sun, not a visible one at any rate, and my father pissed as hell.

Getting old, my father thought.

What he meant was he suddenly could not remember the color of our maid's eyes, all his usual devices for resurrecting memory, from the Latin memoria, coming to naught, and for the first or the second or the hundred twenty-second time in his life he felt himself to be a numskull, a blockhead, in other words a truly stupid person, no matter, but nothing, there was nothing my father detested more than these sudden and inexplicable gaps in his memory, I mean what did these gaps say or do about his interminably long life or even life in general, and in time and with time these gaps, as my father referred to them, were only bound to increase, in other words head in one direction instead of its opposite, and what did that say about the importance or lack thereof of people, places, events and even time itself, to say my father was feeling himself at his wits' end might be an exaggeration but only slightly, of course he could have handled and or solved the issue quickly enough, walked into our maid's room or simply called and had her come to him, in all of his as well as her interminably long lives our maid never failed to answer my father's call, in other words never failed to come to him, but as a solution that would have been too simple as well as simplistic as far as my father was concerned, in other words throughout his interminably long life my father had always preferred complicated as opposed to simple and or simplistic solutions, with a few notable exceptions of course, and in this case the simple solution would have been to call our maid and look into her eyes instead of try to recollect their color ex nihilo as it were but my father not my father for nothing, in other words he preferred misery in the absence of a complicated solution to relief in the presence of a simple one.

And.

If he couldn't recall the color of our maid's eyes, what else couldn't' he recall?

You see the problem, of course.

Nearing the end of time my father as if already losing out to it. He clenched his fists.

Grasping what? He couldn't say. Or wouldn't.

'What's the matter?' our maid asked as she was passing by.

Which she often did of course without looking up, that is directly into my father's face, his eyes, in other words without revealing the true color of hers.

No matter. But.

'What's on your mind?' she asked. And then.

Yes, then she did look up, and her eyes emerald or sea green, in other words brilliantly, although not quite, but nearly brilliantly transparent, and 'Ah, at last, at last,' my father sighed, which our maid didn't even try to comprehend, I mean if she had tried to comprehend everything my father thought or said or did she would have been some kind of mess for sure, and then my father simply smiled and shrugged, tried to embrace her in fact, but on this as on all other occasions our maid simply slipped from his grasp, 'Not so fast, Charlie,' she said, on certain occasions our maid calling my father Charlie even though of all his names that had never been one, and 'Must you?' my father asked, meaning if not this, what, and if not now, when, but our maid with the sea or emerald green eyes simply stepped back while still, and this is important, still keeping her eyes on him.

'You are my love,' my father said. Then, I mean.

And this was the first time he had said that to her, used that particular word I mean, although there may well have been other times to others in the past, but for argument's and or romance's sake let's just say there weren't, but by now my father must have figured if nothing else worked why not this, I mean he had everything to gain and nothing to lose, which was one way to look at it of course, it certainly was.

Our maid took her time.

Which she nearly always did of course, at least as far as my father was concerned

She took her time.

'What else?' she finally asked.

In other words what else was there or was that all my father had to say. To which my father had no reply.

Of course.

Stood there simply smiling and shrugging. 'How time does fly,' he finally managed.

The best, under the circumstances, the best he could come up with. Good enough?

Hardly. But.

Just then or somewhat later.

Our maid took what can only be described as pity or pity for pity's sake on him.

More or less.

And.

'It's all in your mind, Charlie,' she said. A tautology if my father ever heard one. 'You bet your sweet ass,' my father said. Both of them smiling by then.

And they shook hands and went into their respective corners.

My father whistled a happy tune.

Lucked out beyond his wildest imagination.

He was put in charge of the grandest ferris wheel in all of the city, the authorities' way of keeping him out of or placing him right in the midst of trouble, in other words not my father's concern, but, 'The ferris wheel just the thing', he told our maid, he even gave it a name, 'The Contractor,' no rhyme or reason, he just did, and for awhile, and here again time not of an absolute but only a relative importance, but for awhile my father the happiest man in the world, in his own eyes as well as those of others', in other words my father liked nothing better than greeting then taking the kids by the hand and leading them inside one of the cars that appeared to be a miniature version of the single streetcars that cruised the city, only the former went up then down instead of straight and across, in other words we're talking of circular not linear motion, and it was well known that along with Aristotle as well as Newton my father preferred circular to all other motions or that of all motions he detested linear the most, no matter, at any rate his love contagious, after just a single ride all the kids loving circular and detesting linear motion, most of them lined up for second, third and even fourth rides, in other words they could not get enough of both the ride and my father, or, 'Once is not enough,' as my father put it to them and later to me, and this is without any mention of the views of the city, the higher the cars rose the more the kids saw, until at the very top they saw the very boundaries of the horizon, glimpsed the very curvature of space, and, 'What did you see?' my father asked them as they left the cars, his exit interviews as it were, and for those who could not or would not reply readily my father provided the words, in other words transposed reality into symbols they could all comprehend, and it was this, exactly this that eventually got him into trouble, I mean where did a common ferris wheel man come off talking about space and time to innocent and impressionable kids, this was the state's role and no one else's, my father eventually arrested and brought up on charges of corrupting the young, like Socrates he was given the choice of exile or death by suicide, and, also like Socrates, he chose the latter of course, for given his past experiences he was fairly sure of retuning from death but not so from exile, as a method he chose imbibing three bottles of corked Bull's Blood, his favorite wine, sure to kill even a man of my father's enviable constitution, upon completion he burped to his heart's content and promptly entered a death-like, dream-like state, he floated miles above the city before gently landing on the balcony of our apartment, 'Just let me know ahead of time the next time you pull a stunt like this,' our maid chided him, but my father still dreaming and or dead, in other words he couldn't have replied even if he had wanted to, and our maid shoved him inside and waited for him to come to life and or his senses, whichever came first.

'Your hearing going,' our maid told my father. Meaning sight, taste, smell and touch as well. But mostly hearing.

In other words our maid finding it increasingly difficult to handle my father, my father a young old man or an old young one as far as she was concerned, in other words what to do, what to do, she said one thing and my father heard another, or she did one thing and my father saw another, or she applied one brand of perfume and my father smelled another.

And all the while my father like a bear or bull in mating season, 'Keep your paws off of me you damn dirty ape!' our maid often misquoted her favorite line from her favorite movie at the time, all in good fun of course, but fun was fun but this, she felt, this something altogether different, in other words she feared for my father's sanity as much as for her own safety, my father as if suddenly way ahead of the game or completely behind, her that is, and it was a good thing our maid was as swift as she was and my father as clumsy as he, in other words she sailed while he trotted, ran while he groped, in his mindless or mindful pursuit my father bumped into all the chairs, tables and even the very walls, 'Remember who you are!' our maid yelled out but of course he couldn't or wouldn't, his memory more or less shot to hell by then, he located an old hunters' horn of his, a gift from his days in the English countryside, and he blew this as he charged, when he tripped and fell he nearly swallowed the instrument, a good thing too or just in the nick of time as they say, and, 'Saved by the horn!' our maid exclaimed, even though she had little use for horns but for bells even less.

But.

Our maid cracked a big one in the middle of the night, in her sleep one can assume but with no absolute degree of certainty, at any rate she farted like there was no tonight or tomorrow for that matter, and depending on one's experiences it sounded either like distant thunder or heavy artillery, but to my father it was neither, in his heightened state of sensitivity and or horniness, and one would do well at this stage to recall the horn he had nearly swallowed, it was nothing less than the call of love, in other words it not only brought him to his senses but resurrected love in its more or less pure manifestation, he slid or slipped or crept to our maid's door, in other words in the crack of a fart or the blinking of an eye he turned from a Cossack into a gondolier, and at our maid's door he listened and longed for more, but, no, that was all or it for the night, no matter, it was time to take matters into his own hands he felt, and as a gondolier what else but to sing, to serenade, and, 'My own,' my father sang, 'let me call you my own,' in some male Deanna Durbin fashion, and, 'Sweet Mary, save me,' our maid from within, and 'God save me,' also from within, but by that time my father as gentle as a lamb although one very much in love, in other words he was perfectly content just to sing, and, 'Can I get you a bromo or an aspirin?' our maid whispered after the song had ended, she meant well of course, but by that time my father preferring the medication of his silence as well as hers to any other sort, in other words my father perfectly happy to spend the rest of the night in silent vigil, guarding our maid's dreams as well as his own perhaps.

My father a semi-amateur variety performer. I may have mentioned this before.

And this is down through the ages I'm talking about.

He did remarkable animal as well as human imitations, a natural mimic if ever there was one, the former nearly always to great acclaim, the latter to apprehensive guffaws and even consternation, 'Careful,' he was warned, 'careful,' but often too late, in other words by the time of the warnings my father had gone too far, but he didn't give a damn, once in the middle of a performance there was no going back he felt, or, 'The show must go on,' he smiled, I'll give just a few examples, at the court of the Great Khan my father did a timeless imitation of Genghis himself, at the Sun King's palace my father portrayed Louis as a bumbling peddler, at the Great Hall of the people my father showed Stalin as a kosher butcher, at the Nuremberg Arena my father pictured Hitler as a drunken bartender, the Beer Hall Putsch and all that.

And these just a few examples as I said,

In other words my father creating and or simply asking for trouble.

'But these are my best materials,' he sighed on his numerous arrests.

He tried escaping of course, ran like the wind immediately after each and every performance, but who could have escaped the Khan's warriors or Louis' soldiers or Stalin's KGB or Hitler's SS?

In other words his situation both serious and hopeless, or serious but not hopeless, or hopeless but not serious.

And.

And this is a curious fact or footnote to history.

My father's so-called trials following his executions. In other words after not before.

Because of adverse publicity one can only assume.

'But how can they try a dead man?' our maid moaned or groaned or simply asked.

My father, the dead man, only shrugged his shoulders. 'What will be, will be,' he said as a dead man.

In other words why worry about spilled beans or lentils or even peas he asked our maid.

His dead body, tried and convicted I might add, unceremoniously dumped in front of our building.

'Good riddance to bad rubbish,' the Khan's warriors, Louis soldiers, Stalin's KGB and Hitler's SS said.

In other words they all said.

Our maid carried his dead body up the stairs. Cradled like an infant in her arms.

'Home now,' she smiled at me, 'he's home at last.' Shed the necessary tears of course.

But then.

Of course.

My father rose from the dead. Hungry as a horse,' he told our maid. Or.

'I could eat a horse.'

Which our maid understood perfectly well.

And, it being wartime, she promptly prepared his second favorite meal of roast horse, which she allowed him to slice himself.

'Sweet,' my father smacked his lips, 'as sweet as all our yesterdays.'

Our maid smiled and nodded.

She always appreciated a kind compliment.

My father with a huge erection.

For the place and time and circumstances.

His being already dead or just barely alive or both dead and alive. He stared down.

'Save the best for last,' he smiled.

He had always fancied dying with a huge erection, or living, or dying and living both.

In other words my father quite pleased with the way things were turning out, in other words pleased with himself.

'Have you ever seen its like?' he asked our maid.

And she had, of course she had, but to please and or humor a living and or dead man she shook her head.

'Ah, if only this could talk,' my father sighed.

Which our maid simply took as a joke in bad taste or a tasteless exaggeration.

'Touch the magic wand,' my father gestured, 'and all your dreams will come true.'

Our maid laughed out loud.

'When you wish upon a star,' my father sang.

In other words at or near or not yet at the end my father simply trying to make sense of things or practice his usual reductio ad absurdum for a final time, he only wished, but the absurdity of his huge erection just one of the many absurdities he had encountered and or lived through, and what he wanted or tried now was to reduce all the absurdities to just this single one, if at all possible, in other words at or near or not yet at the end of his life my father hoping to comprehend it all by understanding as well as appreciating his huge erection, he only hoped our maid would feel the same, an instance of one good thing leading to another, and this at a time when he felt himself running out of instants, in other words time still but not much longer on the side of his huge erection, his huge erection like a rolling stone then without the rolling, 'Come away with me,' he whispered, both to our maid as well as his huge erection, given the state of his body-mind or mind-body it is doubtful he was able to clearly distinguish between the two, no matter, our maid with a good notion to grab him or it to pull him back to life, in other words to cross certain boundaries she had never permitted herself to cross before, but what was a boundary or two among friends she thought, in other words our maid only human and tempted like everyone else, 'Life and more life,' my father whispered, in other words the bottom line or the best he could come up with under the circumstances, and, 'Gee, it's nice after ending your date,' he sang, and it was nothing short of remarkable that under the circumstances he could both still sing as well as maintain his huge erection, our maid not unduly or duly impressed, in fact 'You are right, sir,' she smiled, 'that is one hell of an erection,' and she may or may not have been ready to take it further than that, we will never know, but just then my father leapt to his feet, a compliment, a kind word all he needed to once more embrace life, and then towering, in a manner of speaking, but towering over our maid like a huge erection himself nearly frightened her to death, in other words all her old fears and or misgivings and or hesitations returned full force, perhaps even with something of a vengeance, and once again she thought of that line from her favorite movie at the time but this time she merely thought it without saying it out loud, it was enough, and, 'Later for you, Charlie,' she pushed my father off who could barely, just barely maintain his balance, and off, off she rushed to the haven of her room where on her narrow balcony she inhaled the city's stagnant air, and there she had the presence of mind to whisper a short prayer to the Virgin Mother upon whose completion she immediately burst out laughing, I mean it never failed, after every prayer she spoke or whispered or simply thought our maid immediately burst out laughing.

Which was why my father loved her so.

Or thought he did.

It all depended.

'How many versions of life can be true?' my father asked.

My father not just tone deaf but nearly totally deaf by then, I mean he could still hear what he wanted or absolutely needed to hear but little or nothing else, in other words my father in that peculiarly happy phase of his life where he could substitute his own words and or meanings for those of others', in other words just make things up in an intoxicating mixture of fact and fiction, for example, 'Come here,' our maid said to him which my father interpreted as, 'You are my one true love, Charlie, or, 'Go away,' she said which my father heard as, 'I'll follow you to the ends of the earth.'

And this in the present as well as the past.

In other words my father's memories in leaps and bounds or simply in favor of what might have been, or, 'Show me an individual with a creative memory and I'll show you a happy man,' the way he put it, in other words at this late phase of his life my father once again busy reinventing himself, which was his favorite pastime and or hobby if you prefer.

'Life just a bowl of cherries,' he sang as he spit out the pits. And, 'Cuddle up a little closer,' he sang to whoever would listen.

Somehow or other he rediscovered his old viola da gamba from the seventeenth century, fashioned by none other than Richard Meares of England, and along with this his bass viola da gamba fashioned by Barak Norman, Richard's sometime competitor.

And these in turn, in other words now one, now the other, he began to play once more.

'Come,' he told our maid, 'come, give me a hand.' Or.

'Come, let's make some beautiful music together,'

In other words two were better than one, especially where a viola and a bass viola da gamba were concerned.

In other words my father crazy for music. Especially when he made it.

Or especially when he made it with someone else. 'Just don't break the damn thing,' he warned our maid. Our maid cautious at first.

She didn't know a viola from a creola, not her fault she was just a simple girl from the country, and this through the ages, but she was willing enough to learn, and for once my father with the patience of a natural-born teacher, 'No, no, not between your legs,' he gently chided, in other words he showed her just how to hold it and stroke not strike the strings with the bow, 'Nice'n easy does it,' he kept encouraging, and in time and with time they struck up the 'Marsellaise' quickly followed by 'God save the Queen,' which, again, in time and with time evolved or devolved into a spirited csardas, our maid stamped or stomped her feet, no matter, all the icicles fell off the roof of our balcony, it was the middle of winter, the sun came out, 'Ah, I'll melt your heart yet,' my father sighed, our maid neither agreed nor disagreed, but she played with a gusto equal to my father's, it had the neighbors pounding on our walls, but in his deafness my father only heard the csardas, only what he wanted and needed to hear.

'Pardon me, girl, is that the Chattanooga choo-choo?' my father asked when they were done.

And.

'Track twenty-nine,' our maid nodded and smiled.

In other words.

My father wandered the war torn streets, it was just one foot after the other but sometimes slow, sometimes fast, it all depended, bullets flew and shells exploded, in other words my father fully in his elements, 'Ah, you haven't lived till you have died,' he once confided to me, he was looking for provisions, trading in a bit of horse flesh you might say, in the end he managed half of a skinny rump of a no longer chestnut mare, hoisted then carried it on his shoulder like a sack of flour which was what he was truly after, he dripped blood as he went, the horse's, not his own, in other words he left a bloody trail for anyone to follow, someone did and shot him dead on the spot, if a horse then why not my father, in other words just a simple case of one total stranger shooting another and for just a bit of horse flesh if that can be believed, and clean as a whistle I might add, the bullet going straight through his heart and exiting out back, 'Ac tu, Brute,' my father was heard to whisper in his quote or misquote of whatever Latin remained to him, the stranger of course neither understood nor particularly cared to, and in time and with time my father simply dragged, pulled, carted off like so much horse flesh himself, with the aid of neighbors our maid carried him up the stairs, 'Oh, no, no,' she whispered, 'not again,' by that time our maid growing sick and tired of my father's various deaths and resurrections, I mean she would have preferred just a single death and if absolutely necessary just a single resurrection, they laid him out on the kitchen floor, in other words flat on his back, the wound to his heart absolutely perfect, they all admired it, nothing like a single well aimed bullet at close range, 'Ah, if only,' our maid sighed, she stuck a single finger into the wound, touched my father's broken heart producing a slight tickling sensation, and then the more she touched the more it tickled as far as my father was concerned, his initial smile turned into a grimace and then an out-and-out laugh, 'I'm just a prisoner of love,' he sang out, all present circled around him then waiting to hear more, I mean alive or dead my father had a million of them, but at and for the time that was all, given his latest traumatic experience my father couldn't get beyond, 'I'm just a prisoner of love,' he repeated this over and over and over until everyone grew sick and tired and left him sitting up on the floor, our maid the only one who stayed behind and pretended to keep listening, but even she, 'Can't you sing another tune?' finally remarked, but my father couldn't, I mean under the circumstances nothing, meaning nothing else would come to him, 'I'm just a prisoner of love,' he sang late into the evening and part of the night while our maid applied cold compresses to his head, heart and gonads, the very sources of the song as far as she could figure.

It was only towards dawn that my father finally came up with another song, 'I can't give you anything but love, baby,' at which our maid shut her eyes and promptly fell asleep.

To mourn my father's death, his numerous deaths, our maid let her hair grow long.

Gold and silken or dark and coarse depending on the circumstances. It was down to the small of her back by the time she decided to cut it. And then.

She decided to donate her hair to charity, a cancer hospital for children not far from our home, I mean not having any children of her own our maid simply wanting to bring a smile to those of others', in other words the bald and sickly and or dying children of others', by her own and my father's calculation her long hair sufficient to cover the bald heads of at least two dozen children, 'Ain't nothing like the real thing, baby,' my father sang as our maid left our apartment with her hair, made aware in advance of our maid's arrival the hospital administrator along with a number of his staff and some of the ambulatory children greeted her by the door with a little impromptu ceremony, 'Greater love than this no woman has who gives her only begotten hair to the least of these little ones,' a few of the children fainted but were efficiently and sufficiently revived, the administrator delivered a short speech, or long, extolling the virtues of sacrifice in general and self-sacrifice in particular, more kids fainted and had to be revived, from the inside pocket of his white jacket he pulled a golden star, fake not real, which he tried to pin on our maid's coarse jacket, it didn't work, in the end he simply had to hand it to her, 'Do you know the one about the blind prostitute?' our maid asked, in other words by then our maid infected by my father's odd sense of humor, our maid finally given the keys to the various cancer wards, she could come whenever she wanted, bring a guest if she felt like, 'Wait till he hears about this,' she smiled, the children sang a chorus from 'The Sound of Music' or was it 'My Fair Lady,' which they had been rehearsing ad nauseam to have ready whenever the occasion demanded, single file they marched back into the hospital, the stronger supporting the weaker or the other way around perhaps, 'Now, how about some nice oatmeal and raisins?' the administrator asked, but by that time our maid ready to move on, she used my father who needed some tending to as an excuse, but all in all it was a lovely day in spite of the gusty winds and menacing clouds which made our maid run like the dickens to avoid getting soaked to the bones.

My father alone in a bare room with his interrogator.

My father in the light and his interrogator in the shadows. In other words my father seen without being able to see.

His interrogator faceless, ageless and perhaps even genderless. None of which bothered my father of course.

He had had dealings with faceless, ageless and even genderless interrogators before.

'Who made you?' a voice asked.

'God made me,' my father responded without hesitating. 'And why did God make you?'

'To love and serve Him in this life and be forever happy with Him in the next.'

The personal pronoun bothered my father of course, whenever he thought of God which was rarely if at all, it was neither as a person nor a pronoun, no matter, my father willing to abide by whatever rules of the game he was asked to play.

And then.

Something.

An odd thing happened.

The bare bulb directly above my father's head reminded him of the sun, in other words suddenly he could no longer distinguish it from the sun, one and the same as far as my father was concerned, and, 'The sun,' he quite naturally pointed and remarked, and these simple words as well as his gesture threw the proceedings into disarray, the questions ceased and or were replaced by an ever increasing humming noise, my father not unnaturally took this for swarming bees, 'Ah, the bees, the bees,' he mumbled, the unknown interrogator stormed from the room, 'But must you leave so soon?' my father shouted after him, in other words if my father couldn't make head or tail of his interrogator, neither could his interrogator make head or tail of my father, the whole thing a bust in the end, my father released on his own recognizance along with his damned sun and swarming bees.

He meandered through the streets before heading for home. 'You all right?' our maid asked.

'Never better,' he replied.

'Let me make you some tea with honey.'

The color of the tea and the taste of the honey reminded him.

'Come away with me,' he sighed as he sipped. 'I promise you the taste of the sun and the warmth of honey.'

He got them mixed up of course. Understandable under the circumstances. 'And where shall we go?' our maid asked. Or.

'Shut up and drink your tea.' Or, and finally.

'Give it a rest, old man.' Which my father understood.

He drained his cup and asked for another.

My father compiled a list. Two columns.

The past and the present. The left and the right.

In other words the things that had already and those that were still to happen.

Certainties and possibilities in other words. The present left out in other words.

Because who could make a list or even sense of the present?

In other words my father's list his half or full-hearted attempt to tackle time once again.

Definitively or not.

He wrote in his meticulous Carolingian script, in other words took his time in dealing with time, and this he accompanied by a selection of Gregorian chants which he sang off key in his cracked but impressive baritone.

In other words.

The apartment filled with music once more. And.

The list grew longer and longer as night followed day and day the night before.

My father after some sort of correspondence between events of the past and those of the future, a kind of symmetry even if he had to fake and or create it.

It was the poet as well as the scientist in him.

"Why did the apple fall from the tree?' he asked our maid during one of his infrequent breaks.

'To knock some sense into your head, of course,' she replied without batting an eye.

And.

The list grew longer.

'I'm not wearing any underwear,' my father blinked at our maid during one of his infrequent breaks.

Which our maid found at once strange as well as amusing.

Because the fact was my father never wore any underwear, and this down through the ages I'm talking about, with the exception of his long johns of course on his various climbing exploits on different continents.

Yes.

No.

My father liked it loose and hanging in other words, unencumbered and ready for action.

'I'm not wearing any underwear,' he repeated. 'So?' our maid looked at him. 'Neither am I.' Which nearly drove my father crazy.

'Just we two, if they knew,' my father sang.

In other words temporarily substituting a popular show tune for his seemingly endless Gregorian chants.

The list finally finished. Or not.

In a small ceremony for one my father took the reams of paper down to the park in the middle of the night.

Where he burned them.

'To light up the night,' as he later explained.

In other words turning words into flames, thereby fusing as well as destroying both the past and the future.

On his return our maid served him his favorite midnight snack. Pig's knuckles and garlic toast.

'Won't you join me?' he asked her.

But just then our maid with an upset stomach or head or heart, and she politely refused.

My father faked amnesia.

Yet another of his attempts to tackle what he felt was his imprisonment by time.

'I remember nothing,' he told our maid, at which she shook her head and smiled.

'And who are you?' he stared deep into her eyes. 'An enchantress, no doubt. Tell me. Have we met before?'

'Several times. By the shores of the Amazon, the Nile, the Danube if I'm not mistaken,' she replied. 'But those were so long ago I can barely recall them myself.'

Two can play this game, our maid must have been thinking. 'And we were lovers,' my father prompted.

Our maid hesitated.

'Sometimes yes, sometimes no.'

My father tried to seize her about the waist.

In other words his attempt to focus on the yes-es rather than the no-s. Our maid slipped from his grasp.

'Seize the day,' my father pleaded as became a man faking his amnesia. 'Something's burning,' our maid drew back.

'Of course, of course,' my father assured her. 'My heart, your heart, our hearts.'

Our maid rushed off into the kitchen to tend to her veal ragu.

No longer certain of anything, which he never was of course but now less or more than ever, my father joined a carnie.

A traveling circus of sorts.

They were glad to have him of course, my father still something of a commanding, striking figure, 'A touch of needed class,' as the owner confided to his troupe, at any rate my father still with an enviable balance as well as the strength of ten, twenty or even thirty, in other words he could not only perform various acrobatic and or high wire acts but bend iron bars and or break steel chains by the sheer expansion of his chest, and when called upon hawk the show, beat the drums and introduce the various acts, because of his sheer size and peculiar sense of humor he made a better than adequate clown, had them rolling in the aisles as they say, his various pratfalls did no greater damage than dislocate his shoulders, arms and crack a few ribs on either side of his torso, he soon enough recovered the way he always had under similar circumstances in the past, in other words my father game for just about anything to entertain, to please, to out-and—out amaze, in the course of the year my father traveled with the carnie the owner gave him monthly if not weekly bonuses, 'Spend it on the women,' the owner winked, 'the flying beauties, the midgets or the bearded lady if that's your preference,' all of the above with a thing for my father needless to say, in other words my father never had to spend a dime for favors sought and more than willingly bestowed, in time and with time my father christened Casanova after the famous or infamous lover of reality and or legend, Casanova the Hawker, the Strong Man, the Trapeze Artist or the Clown, it all depended on the town, the night and my father's various and varying performances, but more than anything else or above all other things my father preferred working with the animals, there appeared to be an immediate and nearly incomprehensible connection, between my father and the animals that is, and these included dogs, chimps, horses, as well as your omnivorous and or carnivorous beasts, lions and tigers and bears I'm talking about, in other words all that was required was for my father to gaze and or stare into their eyes and vice versa for the establishment of what you might call an unbreakable bond, in other words in time and with time my father the animals' lord and master, and this without the use of whips, chairs or any other instrument of aggression, needless to say all so-called unbreakable bonds breakable in the end, no rhyme or reason, they just are, during one unfortunate performance in some nameless town on the shores of the Tisza my father's favorite lion leaped and then mauled my father to yet another of his apparent deaths, the audience gasped but not without thoroughly enjoying the spectacle, a local ambulance rushed my father to the nearest hospital and or morgue where our maid eventually arrived to collect him, 'Did I or did I not tell you that playing with pussies would be the death of you yet,' she whispered into his ears, but of course it wasn't, not then or not yet, and once more my father rose from the dead, or if my father knew how to die our maid certainly knew how to resurrect him, 'Take me home,' my father sighed, 'take me home now,' but our maid took her time, no doubt she meant to teach my father a lesson, but over the many centuries of his existence my father had learned exactly as many lessons as he had managed to forget, in other words the chances of it sticking this time practically nil, so in the end our maid simply shoved my father into a neighbor's pickup truck and drove him all the way home, hoping at least for the bumpy ride to knock some much needed sense into my father's stubborn skull.

She didn't slow for school zones, railroad crossings, stop signs and or red lights flashing or not.

Drove him straight home in other words. Set all sorts of records.

'Memory a curious thing,' my father once confided to me. Or.

'Make sure your umbrella is upside down.' Or.

My father full of memorable last words, his so-called dying confessions. For example.

As a mortally wounded gladiator in the Coliseum he was heard to shout to Augustus himself, 'Stay away from raw cabbage!'

For what it was worth. And.

On the torture rack during the Spanish Inquisition he smiled at Tortumega and politely inquired, 'Does your mother know what you do for a living?'

And.

About to be strung up in one of Hitler's concentration camps my father looked down at one of the guards and said, 'Rope, for God's sake, rope not wire!'

And other examples of course, too numerous to mention.

And once to our maid when he appeared to be definitively dying in her arms, 'A fine romance,' he sang.

'With no kisses?' she immediately smiled back.

Which was just the thing my father needed to leave death to the dying and life to the living.

In other words he was up and at'em in no time. 'But won't you nestle?' he asked.

'No,' she smiled, 'not even wrestle.'

In other words our maid knew just how to handle my father, to give him something to live for.

'Ah, I'd walk a million miles,' my father smiled.

Which during his interminable life he probably already had. Our maid held him in her arms.

'Are we cuddling?' my father asked. Our maid made a noncommittal gesture.

'Tell me,' my father insisted, 'are we cuddling?'

'You're a putz,' our maid smiled.

My father had no choice but to smile back.

My father entered hostile territory.

'Hell,' he later told me, 'the only word to adequately describe.' Where? When? How?

My father purposefully vague in his various recollections and or descriptions.

'Think of robots,' he elaborated. Somewhat.

'Think of robots acting as human beings.'

Or of human beings acting as robots he could just as easily have said. 'Thoughtless,' he added.

Which he almost never or nearly always was. It all depended.

He made a gesture to create as well as negate the terrain. In other words to create as well as negate time itself.

'Hedge rows,' he continued, 'we moved along the hedge rows.' In other words.

Shot at and shooting back. How many casualties?

Wounded and or dead?

My father refusing certain details.

His entire story hanging in the balance. The balance of the missing details. 'Afterwards.'

Silence then.

Before and after but not during.

'Afterwards,' my father finished, 'we drank champagne from our canteen cups.'

'And that's all?' our maid asked.

'What more do you want?' my father smiled at her. The two of them walked off into the sunset.

In other words our maid walked into her kitchen and my father for a turn around the block.

My father noticed a woman sitting on a pillar by the river's edge.

All women beautiful from the back he thought and some, quite a few from the front as well.

He meant to ascertain, to discover.

It was one of those incredible dawns or evenings or the dead of night.

In other words my father my father, the woman the woman and the place the place.

Time the only uncertain variable.

My father positioned himself in front.

In other words facing the woman but not the river. The river to his back.

The woman looked up or didn't. Hard to say.

Stared right through my father perhaps.

'And what is a gorgeous creature like you doing all alone on a night like this?' my father asked.

Or dawn or evening. It all depended.

The woman heard without seeing.

In other words hearing but not yet seeing.

'Counting my blessings,' the woman replied to the ground.

Now, my father still and always a mathematician of course with few if any equals when it came to counting and or adding things up.

In other words in time his timing impeccable. So.

'Recently a computer came up with the largest whole number divisible only by itself,' he told her.

The woman not exactly impressed.

In other words still just hearing without seeing. Still.

'You're blocking my view,' she said.

Of the river she meant or the light or the darkness. My father dressed in his hunter's uniform.

Or his soldier's.

His butcher's.

Or his white laboratory gown.

'Ah, but what do you say?' my father smiled.

Meaning how about I take you away from all this or what's a nice girl like you doing in a place like this.

Anyway?

At which the woman did look up. Finally.

Seeing my father for what he was or might have been.

In other words seeing my father as a hunter or soldier or butcher or, most likely, a half-baked professor of all the sciences that ever were.

'But can you sing?' she asked. 'Can I sing?' my father gestured.

And he immediately started the well known Russian ballad about the woman who had lost her love and or herself.

His grating baritone carried across the river and back. Boomeranged.

Hit the woman like a slap in the face. 'Jesus,' she exhaled.

But.

Once begun my father hardly ever stopped, his strength as well as his weakness, he could carry an off-key tune farther than any man, woman or child alive or dead, to the ends of the world in fact and back again.

'We're just a couple of tots,' my father tried.

In other words exchanging the somber for the light, trying to change the atmosphere, to hit the right note or notes in his off-key fashion.

'You do anything other than sing?' the woman asked in a blasé fashion. At which my father woke up.

Or the woman did.

In other words it was either my father dreaming of this woman or this woman dreaming of my father, little difference either way, the main thing was that either he or she or both of them woke up, realized the futility if not outright impossibility of the situation, in other words just who was trying to enter whose life and thereby alter its course, 'Let's not do this any more,' the woman finally smiled, 'But we've barely begun,' my father objected, at which the woman shoved my father into the river, better his death than her own she must have figured, my father carried quite a ways before he was finally pulled under, keep in mind that in this dream that was no longer a dream my father couldn't or no longer wished to swim, he arrived home with the river's stench on his clothes and flesh, 'Have you been out dreaming again?' our maid confronted him, or, 'Have you been dreaming that you were out again?' she scrubbed him down and promptly put him to bed, 'But won't you join me?' my father still had the strength and or presence of mind to ask, but, 'Just what sort of a woman do you take me for?' she shot back, she pulled his goose down cover well above his head and rocked him to a sleep guaranteed to birth no dreams of suicidal women waiting for him by the river's edge.

My father dead for a long time by then. 'Dust to dust, ashes to ashes.'

Which he wasn't of course, just left in some field to rot, 'Why deny the bugs, the worms a decent meal?' our maid mused during one of her frequent visits, my father wholeheartedly agreed, he got a kick out of watching the bugs and worms busy at work, 'Nothing for nothing,' he told our maid, once again it was the poet as well as the scientist in him, he only wished he could see a bit more clearly and with pen and paper in hand record his careful observations, 'What goes around comes around,' he smiled at our maid, the weather permitting they picnicked in style, in other words joined the feast already in progress, 'All you need is love,' my father mumbled as he devoured our maid's roast duck glazed with apricot jam, in other words they carried on as if nothing or everything had already happened.

'You make a handsome corpse,' our maid said. Small talk appropriate she must have felt. 'Rotting,' my father gestured.

Our maid nodded. How could she not?

'There's always hope,' she smiled as she handed him a drumstick or a thigh or a breast.

The duck's, not hers.

'The wine sour,' my father complained.

Our maid cleaned his lips and tongue of worms and bugs.

My father's great love and or fascination with creatures great and small did not desert him.

'Careful,' he warned, 'careful how you handle them.'

One death at a time quite enough as far as my father was concerned. Especially his own.

Our maid hated to leave him after each visit.

With the ravenous creatures there was no telling how much of him would be left when she returned.

'You've got to have heart,' she whispered to him.

Which my father took as her long delayed but not wholly unexpected confession of her love for him.

'My heart sings like a lark,' my father smiled.

On her next visit our maid brought my father a lark in a bamboo cage. They waited till dawn for the lark to sing.

No dice.

By sunrise the lark stiffer than my father on the bottom of its cage. Dead, in other words.

No matter.

My father good as new.

He and our maid walked back home with my father leading and our maid following.

Our maid refusing to walk beside him.

'My name is Michael, I've got a nickel,' my father sang. Our maid refusing to bite.

She wanted to have nothing to do with my father or his song just then.

My father carried on.

In other words he hopped on his bicycle.

This was after a prolonged period when he slipped in and out of a coma, in other words untouched, touched, untouched then touched again by time, his condition baffled all the doctors, 'Time neither his friend nor his enemy,' one of them shook his head, in other words they simply could not make up their minds, 'But is there nothing to be done?' our maid wrung her hands in a semi-theatrical fashion, acting in her blood, it must be mentioned, nearly as much as in my father's, it wasn't so much the coma she objected to as his constant slipping in and out of it, in other words my father was either alive or dead to the world and why in heaven's name couldn't he make up his mind, 'These things take their own sweet time,' another doctor intoned, or, 'There's no telling with these things,' or, 'Only time will tell,' in or out of his coma my father groaned and made an obscene gesture, our maid served plum brandy out of generous tumblers, the prognoses of drunk doctors more reliable than those of sober ones she must have figured.

'Gentlemen, let's not beat around the bush,' she finally told them. 'Will he ever play the tuba or the hunting or the French horn or the viola de gamba again?'

By then the doctors with several twinkles in their eyes. They smacked their lips as they consulted.

'God, let's hope not,' they finally pronounced in unison. Time passed the way it nearly always did.

Does.

And once again with or without its aid my father as good as new, he looked about the apartment and either liked or disliked what he saw, impossible to tell, and, 'Here we go,' he said and hopped on his bicycle.

At the time his bicycle as red as certain sunsets over the river, over the years, the centuries he'd had others of course but this his favorite, it was a Schwinn of course given to him by a German soldier for dying the good death, in other words shot in the back while trying to make a run for it, 'Here, you need this more than I,' the corporal told the corpse while covering it with the bicycle like a blanket, he even attached a horn to warn the living as well as the dead, 'Now ride, you Jew bastard,' he whispered into the corpse's, that is my father's ear, 'ride like the wind,' after his so- called resurrection my father remembered those words, or those words much needed sources of inspiration depending on the circumstances.

And.

'Oh, what a beautiful morning!' my father sang out. And hopped on his bicycle.

'Where to?' our maid shouted after him.

And.

'Does it matter?' my father shouted back.

In other words he knew a thing or two about bicycles as well as the different routes cutting through the city, but he wasn't about to tell.

His only regret was that it wasn't a bicycle built for two. Schwinn didn't make them in those days.

And.

By sheer accident or pure luck or fate in its multiple dimensions my father rode smack into the May Day Parade, in other words all the flag waving and slogan chanting men, women and quite a few children, my father collided with a buxom blonde from the local fire brigade, practically ran her down, no matter, needless to say it was love at first sight, for God's sake remember the time, the place, the parade and my father's red bicycle, and, 'Could it be you and me, comrade?' my father winked, in other words what or who else under the circumstances, the blonde winked back and promptly dropped out of the parade, and, 'Leave your bicycle,' she whispered, 'you won't be needing it where we're going,' and she led him to the back of the fire station, and there among the ladders, hoses, axes and whatnots of the trade they made passionate love, standing up not lying down as befitted a firehouse, and soon enough the alarms rang, but the fire only metaphysical and or metaphorical, in other words, 'I don't want to set the world on fire,' my father whispered, to which, 'Just shut up and push,' the buxom maid replied, in other words a true daughter of the Revolution if ever there was one, and my father with visions of our maid as he plowed away, in other words he couldn't help himself, nor did he want to.

'Wipe the lipstick off your face,' our maid advised my father after he returned home without his bicycle.

And.

She brushed the blond hairs off his jacket. And.

'All the blondes are whores,' she announced.

With which my father neither agreed nor disagreed. He simply let it go.

My father with an erratic heart. Where? When? Does it matter?

Truth was throughout his interminably long life my father nearly always with an erratic, a tell-tale heart, it's what distinguished him from everyone else, his bum ticker as he called it, it beat now faster, now slower than normal depending on outer and inner circumstances, occasionally he would grab his chest with a gesture worthy of John Barrymore, my father's one- time drinking buddy, 'Hold your horses!'

he'd cry out, meaning the horses galloping or about to come to an abrupt halt, they never did of course, 'You've got the heart of a mule, an ox, a water buffalo,' our maid shook her head, meaning why give her own heart a hard time and possibly break it in the process, 'Just remember who and what you are,' she counseled, which of course neither of them knew or had ever known with any degree of certainty, at which my father gathered, collected or at any rate pretended to partially recognize himself, "let me call you sweetheart,' my father sang, 'Yes, much better,' our maid nodded even as she pushed him away, in other words so long as my father knew or thought he knew who he was his erratic heart could not, would not get the better of him, our maid made him conjugate irregular verbs which at times seemed to have the miraculous effect of regulating his irregular heart, in other words sometimes yes, sometimes no, but all-in-all it worked a lot better than the various pace makers his doctors often talked of installing, 'Over my dead body!' my father thundered, he meant in of course, and 'Over his dead body,' our maid echoed, also meaning in of course, in other words what else but his erratic heart that kept him kicking and alive or alive and kicking all those and these years, in other words the abnormal normal as far as my father was concerned, 'The hummingbird knows best,' my father smiled, by which no one knew exactly what he meant, not even my father himself perhaps, no matter, but when his heart beat fastest he occasionally called our maid his hummingbird, some kind of a connection for sure, 'Who knows?' my father sang, 'Could it be, yes, it could,' to which our maid responded, 'Maybe tonight,' in other words our maid liked or perhaps even loved my father just the way he was, in other words with and because of his erratic heart and not without and in spite of, although for the sake of her own heart and or sanity she always managed to keep him at an arm's distance, and the beats went on in their regular irregular fashion, and this regardless of the dictates of history about which neither my father nor our maid gave a fig, 'How about some figs then?' our maid asked my father, she had gotten them on the black market along with some nylons and Estée Lauder products for herself which she hardly ever used, no matter, my father devoured his figs, cracked them like nuts because in time and with time they had hardened like rocks, 'Let's go for broke,' he smiled at our maid, and, 'How about some more figs?' he asked which he chewed until his teeth loosened and fell out.

And.

My father and our maid walked off into the sunset. Et cetera, et cetera.

My father with greatness rubbed off on him.

Through his various agreeable and or disagreeable associations with the actual great of the past.

I'll cite just one example.

My father Buonarotti's assistant at the height of his powers, Michelangelo's not my father's, my father a kind of go-to guy for the artist flat on his scaffold beneath the Sistine Chapel ceiling, 'Where's my goddamn cup of coffee? Buonarotti shouted and my father scurried like the proverbial ground hog or grayish grouse, it's doubtful Michelangelo even knew his name, my father's that is, he simply called him bum, loafer or bastard, my father that is, for his part my father called the master Boni or Mika but never directly, never to his face of course.

In other words they got along just fine.

Given that no great love was lost between them and only a kind of begrudging admiration on my father's part.

Buonarotti or Michelangelo or Boni or Mika something of a bastard as far as my father was concerned.

A stocky, short-necked bully who lived for nothing but his art. Julius got it right, my father thought.

Buonarotti threw the coffee in my father's face. Or.

Let the cup drop right on top of my father's head. 'You call this coffee?' he thundered.

You with your ridiculous sense of the tragic, my father thought. And this for four years straight.

From fifteen o'eight to fifteen twelve.

Not counting the Last Judgment of course, another seven years much later on.

Savanarola be damned, my father thought, which of course he was by then, burned to a crisp, but the mad monk with an undue influence on the then relatively young Mika as far as my father was concerned.

For God's sake paint a smile on some of those faces, my father thought as he stared up at the ceiling.

Or.

Not everything is hell and damnation or even heaven and redemption. In other words, lighten up, Boni, my father thought.

Still, something there, he had to admit. Possessing and possessed.

At times my father's tell-tale heart beat like a drum as he stared at the prophets, sibyls and the various so-called ancestors of Christ.

Striking if not exactly believable, my father thought.

My father not exactly partial to this primordial vision of humanity. Or.

Let's just say that Michelangelo's conceptions of the heroic leaving a bitter taste in my father's mouth.

And.

Where, oh, where were the women, my father wondered.

He meant the real flesh and blood types and not the pseudo males with boobs attached pin-the-tail-on-the-donkey fashion.

What Mika didn't know about women my father could have taught him, or tried to at any rate.

But.

Not his place of course.

'You call this a frittata?' Michelangelo thundered. But.

My father got his revenge of sorts.

Near the end of his life Boni working on his own tomb in the Cathedral of Florence, imagine that, his own tomb my father shook his head, left unfinished of course and then smashed to bits and reassembled as the saying goes by other hands.

Whose?

My father's of course.

Nothing original, needless to say, but he did come up with a hell of a figure of Magdalen, the whore as saint or the saint as a whore.

My father's idea of two in one as opposed to Michelangelo's nothing in nothing.

My father stared at our maid. 'Can I call you Mary?' he asked.

'You do and I'll break both your arms,' she replied. Not unsweetly.

'Ah,' my father sighed, 'What do you say you wash my feet and dry them with your hair.'

Which by this time had grown back quite abundantly. Our maid told him what he could do with and to himself.

At any rate she would not play Mary Magdalen to my father's Lord and Savior.

'But think of all the fun we could have,' my father persisted.

'Easter coming,' she stared at him, 'I see a cross on Golgotha with your name on it.'

Which was game, set and match as far as my father was concerned.

'Less is more,' my father said, 'More is less.' Which he didn't mean of course, not for a second. But.

By this time the authorities tired of my father's shenanigans, and this is through the ages I'm talking about, I mean they meant to stick him where he would do the least amount of harm if not necessarily any tangible good, my father always with a soft spot for the various downtrodden, rejects of the world, the leftovers of both time and society or the orphans of storms as he put it, the authorities taking this to heart and acting in terribly good faith or bad, the then Minister of Human Affairs placed him in charge of the largest and therefore most notorious orphanage in the country, or, 'Nothing to nothing,' he winked at his secretary, who by some odd coincidence was also a buxom blonde both like and unlike the one from the fire brigade, she took my father aside and after some lovely hanky-panky in the broom closet spoke quite earnestly and or passionately to my father, 'They're truly out to get you this time,' she whispered as well as gesticulated, 'the last dozen directors of The Stable driven both impotent and mad,' The Stable being the name most commonly used for the orphanage, but my father just shook his head and winked, 'How about just one more go in the broom closet?' he suggested, in other words while appreciating the buxom blonde's warning he didn't take it all that seriously or simply had other things on his mind, although that bit about impotence had him worried of course, madness he could and had dealt with most of his long existence but impotence an entirely different matter, 'Sail down the Nile with me,' he whispered to the blonde, he meant up of course, but by this time the blonde summoned to some other more or less pressing duties, and, 'Some other time perhaps,' she waved goodbye and left my father to fate and or his own devices.

Our maid packed a hearty lunch of bacon, onions and multi-grain bread to last for days, weeks or months.

For years perhaps.

'Much may happen ere we see each other again,' she said in her young old-fashioned way.

'You said it,' my father nodded. 'A lot of water under the bridge.' And off, off, off he went.

He traveled by tram, by train, by coach and finally on foot to reach The Stable.

Deep in the heart of the country in other words.

Along the way he told the story of his life any number of times to anyone who would listen in the way of energizing, preparing himself.

'Seven little girls sitting in the back seat, all of them in love with Fred,' he sang to an old peasant who nodded as though he understood.

Or.

'Three coins in a fountain,' he sang to a wizened old woman who loved Sinatra as much as my father did.

The orphans all lined up by the time he arrived.

'Doe, a deer, a female deer,' my father sang as he passed in inspection.

Some of the orphans smiled, nodded while others simply stared into empty space.

'Are we going to have a good time?' my father shouted and the hills or the valley echoed his cry.

They were all there of course.

The scum, the flotsam, the so-called survivors of all the wars, famines, pogroms that ever were, or, 'History on parade,' as my father gestured, he moved now at a brisk pace, now slowly as he inspected them, he gave some cursory glances while with others he stared deep into their eyes, 'Dumbo, you've got to have confidence in yourself,' he told one lanky lad with ears like teacup handles, and, 'The sun will come up tomorrow,' he told a diminutive lass with hair like straw on a dung wagon.

'I'm here on holiday,' he finally addressed them all, 'all of us here on holiday.'

He distributed several gifts.

Mostly field glasses, telescopes and kaleidoscopes.

So they could all see the world in a better or, at any rate, different light. Several of them he enfolded in his embrace.

Practically choking them to death.

'See, it's not so bad,' he whispered and adjusted their field glasses, telescopes and or kaleidoscopes.

'Just open your eyes and see it all.'

Which of course they had for years by then without it doing them much if any good, but my father out to change all that, a kind of Moses or Martin Luther King Junior with some definite notions of the Promised land even though he would not get there himself.

Chances were.

'I could tell you stories,' my father once told me. About Moses for example.

How he and Moses were like this, at which my father crossed two of his fingers, and how if it hadn't been for my father the Lord would have struck the Prophet dead in the desert, and so on and so forth.

No matter.

My father decided to take charge or charged forth decisively.

He organized his charges into groups for self esteem and support, had them marching like Hitler Jugend into the hills and back, minus Hitler of course, taught them several drinking and or revolutionary songs, Broadway and or popular tunes, his charges hardly knew the difference, 'Deep breaths,' he encouraged, 'deep breaths as you sing out,' for sheer entertainment he had them put on shows which he both wrote and directed based on the miserable past as well as the soon to be glorious future,

'Strong, smile, star,' he told them, in time and with time my father and his orphan charges became the talk not just of the surrounding area but of large parts of the country as well, the Minister of Human Affairs quite a bit miffed that my father should have succeeded where others and he himself had failed, in other words my father becoming neither mad nor impotent as the Minister had hoped but saner and ever more potent than ever, stories about my father and some of his older female charges reached his disbelieving ears, whether fabricated or real made absolutely no difference, the Minister felt he had no choice but to shut down The Stable with the orphans scattered to the four winds as it were, my father brought back to the capital, but pronto, to stand trial for corrupting the young, the proceedings broadcast live on radio, 'The best show in town,' everyone agreed, in the end my father sentenced to life imprisonment inside himself the sentence to be carried out immediately, my father retuned home with stars in his eyes and stellar dust all over the rest of him, 'Are we having any fun yet?' my father asked our maid who did her best to get rid of the stars and wash off the dust, They kept her up nights by their annoying glow, but it wasn't until she tried a combination of goose fat, lavender and thyme that the glow began to abate, but even then there were the occasional flashes like distant lights from the original Big Bang of creation.

On several occasions my father tried taking her into his arms, but our maid as adamant in her refusal as she was mistrustful of the light still emanating from my father.

'Cupcake! Butterfly! Ladybug!' my father called out.

In other words my father not about to give up as far as our maid was concerned.

Not yet at any rate.

In other words all he wanted was to show her a good time

He had this idea, this notion of crossing the Pond with our maid by his side, 'What you and I need is to widen our horizons,' the way he put it to her, not that he hadn't crossed the Pond himself before, with none other then Columbus himself as they discovered the so-called New World, 'Chris quite a bastard, you know,' he once told me, 'an unfeeling boob who belonged in a Spanish dungeon and not some Caribbean island,' in other words even though he had been the explorer's sidekick and or navigator my father's revulsion of the man could have filled volumes, 'Never trust the white man,' my father once whispered to me without seeing the irony of his statement, no matter, that was then and this was now, 'Listen, listen to me,' my father pleaded, 'the new world is calling,' by which he did not necessarily mean the New World but a new world, in other words he still hadn't given up trying to get into our maid's panties, 'But what would someone like me do in New York or Washington or Miami?' our maid stared at him, but my father had it all worked out, in the New World or in the new world they would take the low roads not the high, the byways not the highways, he reeled some names off the top of his head, among them Leadville, Rifle, Steamboat Springs and even Salt Lake City, names he thought might appeal to our maid, but, 'Ream 'n Clean is that it?' our maid replied, in other words if she hadn't been taken in by my father's other ruses what made him think she'd be taken in by this one, but, 'In the New World we will love till the rattle snakes, the beavers and the bison come home,' he persisted, in other words did or did not our maid believe that love conquered all in the end, 'Amor vincit omnia,' he even said to her in Latin, to which, 'Why don't you just take me to a downtown bar?' she finally replied, in other words if he truly wanted to show her a good time he might just try something closer to home, 'Right you are,' my father agreed, and he dressed in his spiffiest guard of the watch uniform and she in her gaudiest country skirts and blouse, and off they went to the most elegant and or sleaziest bar he could find, it didn't much matter to him so long as it was warm and dark and conducive to his whispering sweet nothings into her ear, in a place called the Cock and Bull he finally gave it a shot, but, 'You call this a bar?' she countered, and 'You call these sweet nothings?' in other words the waitress surly, the glasses dirty and the table grimy, those things mattered to our maid much more than to my father, and as for sweet nothings they were more nothings than sweet, and what's more she had heard them all before, and once more my father came up wanting, came up short, in other words wanting without getting, and, 'What will it take to melt your cold, cold heart?' my father moaned in boozy frustration, at which our maid placed his arm about her shoulders and dragged him all the way home where she put him to bed without even bothering to remove his spiffy guard of the watch uniform, she sat by his side for a spell and sang him an old country lullaby whose refrains my father clearly recalled in his dreams, then she herself fell asleep and dreamt a most satisfying dream about my father as a young peasant courting her in her father's barn.

And time passed the way it always did. And does.

In other words time embraced them both.

My father picked up his questionnaire.

It was the law of the land which for once he didn't mean to flout. But my father realized of course.

The authorities after the varnished not the unvarnished truth, the tainted not the untainted facts.

For inspiration he worked late at night with the windows wide open.

From time to time he woke our maid to assist with some of the seemingly simple yet to my father trick questions.

'How old am I?' he asked, 'How tall? Are my eyes gray or blue?' Without directly looking at him our maid took wild guesses.

She relished giving herself a certain creative freedom as far as my father was concerned.

'Where was I born?' my father asked. 'When? Do I believe in the Father and the Son and the Holy Ghost or only in the Father or the Son or the Holy Ghost?'

'None of the above,' our maid smiled at him. My father nodded.

'Have I ever been found guilty of bestiality, child molestation, or the rape of one or several Sabine women?'

'In deed or in thought?' our maid asked. My father raised his hands in despair.

'Do I appreciate beauty and or ugliness?' my father asked. 'Both,' our maid replied without hesitation.

'Am I capable of love with or without abandon?' my father asked. 'With,' our maid replied, 'definitely with.'

The moon came up.

My father and our maid temporarily distracted.

'And what of the seeds of my loins?' my father asked.

'Come again?'

'Over the centuries, the eons have I sired multitudes, dozens, or just the one, the current, the single offspring?'

'All of the above,' our maid smiled.

Minutes passed into hours and hours into more hours.

In other words time passed the way it always did and does. And not at all unpleasantly for either of them.

Towards dawn my father finally finished and signed his name to the document.

'A load off my mind,' he sighed.

In other words under the circumstances lies so much better than truths or lies so much more potent than truths.

'Perhaps we should celebrate,' my father looked at our maid. Which they did of course.

With the questionnaire and or document in hand they made for the park where they ceremoniously burned the sheets.

Warmed themselves as if by a bonfire of vanities.

To my father's great delight several naked couples scampered from the bushes in search of safer places in which to give vent to their unbridled passions.

'You and I,' my father sighed.

In other words my father ready for his personal bonfire if only our maid would agree to light the fuse.

'Not here, not now,' our maid smiled. 'Not ever?'

To which our maid did not think it appropriate to reply.

My father growing increasingly abstract in his thoughts, words and gestures.

His mannerisms in other words. Time getting to him perhaps.

I mean had he or had he not been around for centuries, for eons, I mean trapped in the past while he desired nothing but the ever present, 'Have a heart,' he told our maid while he raised his arms and joined his hands in the shape of one, our maid watched from a distance, his most as well as least appreciative audience, my father escaped into impromptu dreams where he attempted to reconstruct the past to somehow coincide with the present, he woke restless and out of sorts, 'Let me count the ways,' he told our maid but even his formidable mathematical skills deserted him on waking, he got no further than three, in other words three ways in which he longed and lusted for her, love of course an entirely different matter which our maid quite rightly recognized, even his voice, such as it was, deserted him, in other words it cracked as he tried for the umpteenth time to sing his way into her heart, our maid filed her nails and painted them as she listened, 'What good is sitting alone in your room?' my father finally managed, to which, 'I'm just a girl who can't say no,' our maid responded, meaning the opposite of course, in other words that she both could and did, 'Some enchanted evening,' my father bellowed, to which, 'Let's take it nice 'n easy,' our maid responded, whereupon my father fell into a deep sleep and even deeper dreams that lasted for several days and nights.

'Don't disturb him,' our doctor cautioned. 'Give him the chance to work things out.'

In his dreams my father moved swiftly through the centuries.

In other words my father attacking time itself and doing his utmost to destroy it.

At times he moaned, groaned and even shouted, while at others he launched into lengthy harangues that sounded like Pentecostal sermons to untold multitudes.

'Blessed are the sinners, the fornicators, the rich in spirit for theirs is the kingdom of earth!' he shouted.

'Rejoice for the hour of the damnation of love is upon us!' he shouted.

Our maid applied cold compresses to his head and wet his lips with a mixture of honey and wine.

'We have nothing to embrace but our bodies,' my father shouted, 'nothing to lose but heaven itself!'

On the third day he rose from the dead. Or as good as the dead.

Awoke and came to his senses in other words. 'Is that lamb stew I smell?' he asked our maid. 'The Pascal Lamb itself,' she winked at him.

And his flesh turned into bread and his blood into wine.

Or the other way around perhaps. All this off the record of course.

Everything about my father's life off the record.

We took shelter in our basement.

From the bombardments of the various advancing and or retreating armies.

At first my father hesitated of course.

His preference for dying in the light rather than the darkness, for dying with his eyes wide open that is.

'But don't you want to see it coming?' my father asked our maid. He meant death of course.

In the end though it was statistics that won the day, our maid counting on my father's great love and respect for mathematics, she quoted the newly formed Homeland Security Office's convincing numbers about deaths from bombardments in apartments as opposed to basements, 'This way, this way,' she said and pushed him out the door, my father, still lightheaded from too much or too little sleep, lacked the strength to refuse, 'But what about my books, my chandeliers?' he vainly gestured, our maid pulled him down the stairs, he nevertheless managed to rush back for his light meter so he could measure the intensity of light from each and every explosion in the basement if at all possible, in the basement it smelled of coal dust and sweat and later of smoke and urine, 'A fine place for a rendezvous,' my father sighed, in the midst of the bombardments he addressed the cowering figures in stentorian tones, in other words he meant for his voice to rival and even rise above the explosions, although one must be careful not to confuse a loud voice with any out-and-out act of heroism, 'Let's embrace uncertainty!' he thundered, 'Uncertainty our salvation and certainty our doom!' it's doubtful anyone understood what he was bellowing, my father's thunderous tones just so many more explosions as far as they were concerned, nevertheless my father once again or still rising to the occasion, in the semi-darkness my father's looming figure like the very Angel of Life or Death depending on one's particular angle of vision, 'I bring you strife not peace, conflict not harmony!' he thundered, 'Please, sit, sit down,' our maid tugged at him, but my father touched by a kind of divine madness by then as he so often was during his interminable years of existence, in other words my father once more overwhelmed by the past while trying to fully embrace the present, or the explosions of the past as if echoing in the present or the other way around, or my father longing for that one, that single direct hit to end it all and start it up from scratch, lowering his voice he delivered a brief lecture on the beginning and ending of time, the expansion and contraction of time, 'Picture a balloon being blown up then bursting apart,' he asked his audience to visualize, not a perfect analogy of course but was he or was he not himself pressed for time, 'The Big Bang just one of the theories,' he tried to explain without undue elaboration, in other words my father painting pictures of a number of possibilities without favoring any single probability, on the whole, in general his audience much more interested in the number of smaller bangs in the present than the possible Big One in the past, in other words the distant past as good as meaningless to them in the lights and sounds of the explosive present, my father needing to cut it short he realized, come up with some sort of grand or even semi-grand finale, 'Gather ye rosebuds while ye may,' he finally shouted at the top of his voice or simply whispered, he didn't know it himself, our maid finally succeeded in pulling him down and throwing a blanket over him, not so that my father couldn't see and hear but so that no one could see or hear my father, it was in this shape or fashion that my father was finally carried upstairs after the melee, in other words my father forced to neither see, hear nor speak any evil, which was never his intention of course, our maid left him in a corner of our apartment until he should come to or totally abandon his senses, it happened sooner or later, my father threw off his blanket and stared wistfully at our maid, 'Ah, but we missed our chance,' he smiled, 'the chance of a lifetime perhaps,' to which, 'What do you say to some nice garlic toast and goose liver?' she replied, in other words our maid fully intending to carry on where they had left off or originally begun, in other words time or no time, beginnings or endings, something simply had to remain the same, my father shook his head and shrugged his shoulders, I mean what else could he do, it was like Passover then, the invading and or retreating armies had passed over our building while destroying a number of others surrounding it, our maid lit a candle and mouthed a prayer of thanksgiving, and finding no bitter herbs or any gefilte fish she served up goose liver and garlic toast.

Plenty of wine of course and or plum brandy. Non-kosher.

And that, precisely, that was why that night was different from all the others.

My father owned a Harley.

One of the first built before the war and perhaps the only one in our part of the world.

'Let me not to the converse of love admit impediments,' my father whispered.

Misquoting of course. No matter.

The Harley a definite impediment.

'Break every bone in your body,' our maid prophesied. 'Ah, let me count the ways,' my father's favorite reply.

In our building's courtyard the Harley taken apart and reassembled any number of times, my father wanting to see just what made it tick and or desperate to mimic its creation, 'We're here for a good time not a long time,' he explained to the stray cats watching from a distance, he tuned, oiled and polished it until it became like a mirror to the sun, he hopped aboard and tore down the street on his way somewhere, nowhere or perhaps everywhere, this initial test run putting the spring back into his steps and the starch into his gonads, 'A fine figure of a man,' our maid had to admit as he walked through the door in his leather helmet, jacket, pants and boots, 'The Nazis' BMWs don't hold a candle,' he gestured, in other words they were neither as light nor as fast as my father's Harley, he had a notion of crossing certain boundaries of time and space which under the circumstances was no longer advisable, 'Just a kind of reconnaissance mission,' he winked and, 'What would it take for you to hop on the back?' he whispered to our maid who simply smiled and shook her head, 'You're missing the ride of your life,' he told her which he meant both literally as well as figuratively or as a double entendre perhaps, our maid could not stifle her laugh, and once again my father realized that more than anything else he was in love with our maid's laughter, it struck as suddenly and unpredictably as lightning, but in the best as well as worst of times my father a realist as well as a dreamer, so, 'Some other time perhaps,' he tipped his helmet and off he rode to the races to the war or whatever else he might encounter.

He crossed rivers, valleys and several mountains, north first then south, in other words having reached the Channel he refused to embark at Dunkirk but headed back down across France and eventually the Pyrenees, but not before a brief stopover at Nice where he generously sampled whatever pleasures remained of life, something he felt he owed himself or simply could not do without, no matter, on his Harley my father either chasing or being chased by death, or was it life perhaps, he was captured, held and interrogated in Barcelona of all places, 'How about cutting me some slack, boys?' he pleaded with the none too friendly SS who did a little dance on his face as well as the rest of him before finally releasing him for lack of enough ammo to kill him with, undeterred my father made it across the Alps and down Italy's boot from where it was just a hop, skip and a jump to Sicily where he awaited the Allied invasion, but here, as so often in the past, my father just a man ahead of himself and or of time, it was on to Yugoslavia and Greece then with its magnificent light and rocky terrain, drunk on ouzo he missed the Parthenon, better luck next time he thought, he turned back at the Bosporus which, drunk as he was, reminded him of the river Styx, at any rate he was ready neither for the Black Sea nor the Sea of Marmara, dodging military transports he made his way up through Bulgaria and Rumania, he arrived back home just in time to stop our maid from cutting her hair in another act of mourning his loss, 'One of these centuries you'll be the death of me yet,' she stared at him, which of course was the perfect cue for starting my father on one of his endless meditations, this time about life in death or death in life, 'I dare you to separate the two,' he stared at our maid, she raised her arms in despair but my father not done yet, 'All my life I've been chasing one or the other or both,' our maid cleared her throat, 'but now all I want is to live or die in your arms,' he continued, 'You decide,' 'Is that all you really want?' our maid smiled, to which my father nodded like the proverbial dog on strings, she took him into her arms where my father neither lived nor died of course but persisted in a state of suspended animation for several minutes, hours or even days, 'All right, all right,' our maid finally had to push him off, 'there's work to be done,' and she proceeded to dust all the furniture, mop the floors and clean all the windows, wartime no excuse for a messy apartment as far as she was concerned, because of an acute food shortage my father trapped some pigeons in the park for our midday meal but in the end neither he nor our maid had the heart to wring their necks, and we all watched as they flew wildly out the sparkling clean windows.

My father took long walks with Einstein.

This was in Princeton of course where my father spent quite a few years in semi-seclusion, from the moment the physicist laid eyes on my father he took quite a shine to him, it may have been my father's walk or the way he mumbled to himself, 'Call me Al,' Einstein told him and broke into step, other than Gödel my father Einstein's favorite walking companion, he regularly accompanied the great man to and from his so-called laboratory which was little more than a bare office where Einstein sat and meditated, or, 'My mind my laboratory,' as Einstein told my father on more than one occasion, 'Right you are, Al,' my father nodded, but Einstein liked Kurt's company for what he said and my father's for what he didn't, in other words by then and in Einstein's presence my father a great listener, 'Walking with you is even better than walking by myself,' Einstein confided to my father, 'Kurt gets me all worked up, wound up with his theories of inconclusive sets and mathematics that don't correspond to reality,' I think it's fair to say that by his silence my father touched something in Einstein just as by his endless talk Einstein touched something in him, 'You see, my friend,' Einstein once halted as did my father, 'in the end reality may be something we're incapable of putting into any system, in other words of truly comprehending,' and this, yes, this was as close to a moment of truth my father would ever experience, the weather often inclement, gusts and rains often accompanied their walks and conversations, 'It clears the head,' Einstein gestured, neither man seemed to mind the elements although my father a bit more than Einstein, but after awhile even my father went sockless in imitation and or tribute to the physicist, Einstein nodded in approval, 'Never think what others think, do what others do,' he smiled, my father mesmerized by the great man's eyes, they reminded him of our maid's although the two looked nothing alike, on one, just a single occasion Einstein invited my father into his office, his so- called laboratory, without any introductory words he proceeded to play a Bach cantata on his violin, 'It used to be Mozart, you see,' he explained afterwards, 'but now it's nothing but Bach,' he expected my father to understand as well as appreciate, 'Mozart is the master,' Einstein went on, 'but Bach, only Bach is the true genius,' my father expected great things of this one and only visit to Einstein's so-called laboratory, the secrets of the universe unraveled, demonstrated through chalky figures on the immense blackboard that served as one of the walls, but Einstein did no more than play his Bach cantata then talk about Bach's music as well as the man and his times, 'A mysterious creature,' Einstein mused, 'as we all are perhaps, but with this all-important difference, Bach fully accepted mystery and so the simplicity of his being as few others have before or since, and it was out of this mystery as well as simplicity that he created, which is the only possible, the only worthwhile creation, everything that goes for so-called creation nowadays is nothing but repetitious nonsense, in which I include myself, as far as I'm concerned if you can't create out of both a mystery as well as a simplicity you're better off not attempting to create at all, you're better off just observing and listening the way you do, no offense,' none taken of course, 'sooner or later every man arrives at a state in his life when he seems to have out lived life itself, lost his initial gift, his very being which consisted of nothing but this mystery and simplicity, and once lost any amount of effort is useless, in fact detrimental in trying to get it back, just look at me,' Einstein gestured, 'nothing,' Einstein regarded my father, 'trust me, there's nothing but brutal honesty in the end, and even that's of no help or any sort of consolation, but, believe me, it's a lot better than lying to oneself, nearly all the human, all the manmade ills of the world can be attributed to nothing but lies to ourselves, what made Bach so great is that he managed to safeguard, to hang on to his gift for as long as he had, but perhaps in the end he too arrived at nothingness, where in his refusal to lie to himself he had to stare nothingness square in the face, and now, my good friend, if you don't mind I would like to be alone, we've grappled together enough I should think,' and my father left without another word being uttered, Einstein certainly with a way of enlightening as well as upsetting my father, no telling which the greater, and my father never more fulfilled nor lonely and insecure than when he left the physicist's so-called laboratory, and walking alone in the inclement weather he could think of, picture nothing but our maid, and the longing in his heart and mind and gonads nearly drove him crazy then, to the very edge of lunacy in fact, and when he finally returned home, re-entered his own life in other words, he nearly scared our maid half to death by his disheveled appearance, 'Look at you,' she could only exclaim, 'my God, just look at you!' she quickly handed him a steaming cup of rum and tea, half and half, which he swallowed in a single gulp, 'Better?' she asked, and my father nodded and smiled the way he so often did in our maid's presence.

And.

'What is it you really want?' our maid asked my father. And.

'To live and die in your arms,' he replied without hesitation. In other words both.

And.

Our maid with no great trust in my father's words, neither in the man himself nor in his words but more in the man than his words perhaps, so, she asked him to elaborate, to make things absolutely clear to her as well as to himself, and this my father couldn't or wouldn't do, his mistrust of words as well as of himself only slightly less than our maid's.

So.

'Ah, just wait till the sun shines, Nellie,' he sang instead. 'You mean by and by?' she asked.

'Yes, precisely,' he nodded, 'by and by.'

It was early or late spring, or early or late summer, or fall or winter.

By then the seasons having little to do with my father, little influence on his activities in other words.

Not so our maid.

Our maid still caught in the seasons, her very moods and activities dictated by their changes.

'Do I love you,' my father sang, 'do I?' 'But it's snowing outside,' our maid replied. Or raining or sleeting or gusting.

Or unbearably hot.

Or the river frozen that winter. That may well have been it.

And.

'Let's take an old-fashioned walk,' my father suggested.

And he waited until our maid donned her boots, her heavy coat and Riding Hood scarf, although for the life of him he couldn't get her to sing, 'Who's afraid of the Big Bad Wolf?' no matter, the red would look terrific against all that white, and off they went.

My father with this notion of crossing the river on foot, all the bridges destroyed, useless by then but a crossing still possible, in other words what remained but to cross from one side of the river to the other and then to continue, to go on for as long and as far as possible, my father walked ahead and our maid behind or our maid up ahead and my father behind, no matter, the main thing was that not even halfway across our maid stopped, froze on the frozen surface, 'Enough is enough,' she stared at my father, 'I'm turning around, heading back now,' because of the biting cold my father in no mood to cajole, to argue or even try to explain, 'As you wish,' he simply shrugged his shoulders and continued on by himself, in other words he headed in one direction and our maid in another, and for the umpteenth time in their long lives they parted company, in other words as often as they had met before they also and inevitably parted, on the far side of the river my father hugged the shore and proceeded up or down along its banks, he was simply biding his time by then or looking, searching for someone to follow, it wasn't long before he saw the figure of a woman in the distance, the woman walking neither slower nor faster than my father but at just about the same pace, in other words it was no one he would ever catch up to and so meet or possibly even recognize, my father sick and tired of meeting new people by then or of recognizing old ones from the past, in other words at this stage of his life he was more than ready to follow someone he would never meet and or possibly recognize, 'That's it,' he even mumbled to himself, 'that's it,' my father sick and tired by then of this game of identities, all identities, no matter whose, were mistaken identities as far as my father was concerned, in other words by then it seemed impossible for my father to recognize let alone truly know anyone else, better the perfect stranger who would remain the perfect stranger for all time, so my father neither slowed nor quickened his steps but kept it in perfect coordination with the woman's up ahead, and if it hadn't been for the bitter cold and the biting winds who knows how long he would have followed her, to the ends of the world perhaps provided she was heading there herself, but all dreams, notions nothing but impossible dreams and notions in the end, so he crossed or recrossed the river, what else could he do, frozen stiff by the time he returned to our apartment, without uttering a single sound our maid stuck him into a hot tub where he gratefully submerged himself to surface only now and again for a deep breath, 'Scrub your back?' she asked, but, no, he preferred to remain submerged and come up only occasionally for a gulp of air, our maid tempted to join him, our tub large enough, but in the end she simply sat and watched and now and then ran some hot water to keep my father's bath from cooling off.

Mistaken identities haunting my father throughout his interminably long life.

In other words my father mistaken for who he wasn't and my father mistaking others for who they weren't.

Which is how he wound up on the last transport to Auschwitz.

'Just a minute, boys, just a minute,' he argued with the guards. 'Are you sure you've got the right customer?'

My father the near perfect Aryan specimen but one that could and was easily mistaken for a Jew.

Our maid saw him off.

The package of sausages and bread she meant to hand him for the journey confiscated by one of the guards.

No windows on the cattle cars.

Our maid couldn't even wave good bye.

As usual, as always my father took his bearings in the semi-darkness. 'Are we having a good time yet?' he asked of the men, women and children squeezed in all about him.

His question, if that's what it was, or joke, if that's what it was falling on deaf and soon to be dead ears.

In other words my father breaking the first rule of comedy, know your audience.

Nevertheless.

He persisted.

The way he had throughout much if not most of his life. 'Are we there yet?' he asked.

In other words my father in the midst, in the very heart of a whole heap of mistaken identities, and this included not just those in the cattle car but the guards riding on top, in other words no one understood who or where or why, but my father up against fluid and or changing and or impossible identities before, in other words he had learned his lesson about the impossible creeping up on and choking, drowning him, and then, as so often before in the past, he simply made up his mind to get the hell out of Dodge, to head for the valleys, the hills, the rivers, the towns, whichever came first, I mean he had no idea, and the thing about my father, once he had made up his mind about something, about anything at all he immediately acted, in other words thinking and acting for him practically the same, and he fell to the floor, not easy in the midst of that pressing crowd, but he did, and tapped and scratched and felt until he found what to him seemed an appropriate, in other words loose plank or planks of the floor, and then he went to work, and in time and with time he had a gap wide enough for a man or a woman or child to slip through, and, 'Follow me!' he yelled or whispered or somewhere in between the two, and once again in time and with time he lowered, eased and eventually dropped onto the tracks, the rest academic of course, the train passed over with my father under, and then, and then he ran for the woods because they were there, shots rang out of course but my father an excellent runner when his life depended on it, as it often did, and he made it even if others after him did not, in other words in this case no safety in numbers, just the opposite, but eventually, in other words in time and with time he arrived at some house or hut or Holiday Inn in the middle of nowhere, which was always his preference, where a woman took him in, 'My, but aren't you a fine looking Aryan,' she said, or Jew, it doesn't matter, the main thing was she took him in, and he spent the remainder of the war in her company and or bosom, 'Let me count the ways,' he often said to her which she didn't or pretended not to understand, but for all that she was a loving and generous soul, with the madness over she sent him on his way, my father bowed and kissed her hands, 'I have nothing but respect for you,' he mumbled, and, 'Good riddance,' she waved goodbye, and it was in this fashion he made it back home, in other words none or just a little bit worse for the wear, and our maid undressed, washed then dressed him once more, in other words restored him to his former self, and, 'Ah, this problem of mistaken identities will be the death of you yet,' she sighed, but still they managed to walk into the sunset together, to the accompaniment of Miklos Rozsa's soundtrack I should add, and, 'Just direct you feet,' my father sang, 'to the sunny side of the street,' with his voice as cracked, as unbearable as ever.

But.

'Don't think this changes anything between us,' our maid warned. At which my father smiled and shrugged his shoulders.

'Make yourself useful,' our maid told my father. Which he wasn't by then, not by a long shot.

That is if he ever had been throughout his interminably long life. By then.

My father with an annoying way of moping, of wandering about the apartment, he moved from room to room, nook to nook as if looking, searching for something, our maid handed him his brand new glasses which only clouded his vision, in other words brought things either too close or too far for any sort of clarity of vision, our maid convinced he had lost, mislaid or forgotten something, 'Give me a hint,' she asked, 'is it smaller or bigger than a shoe box?' my father simply shook his head, at our maid's suggestion my father shoveled coal, beat carpets in the courtyard, and neutered all the strays in the neighborhood but still that glazed, that blank look in his eyes, 'The times they are a changing,' was the only explanation he could offer, he loaded his cavalry pistols and stuck them in the belt of his housecoat, in this fashion he paraded up and down the street in front of our building as if on some kind of improbable sentry duty against all comers, 'You're fooling, scaring no one,' our maid advised, 'except yourself perhaps,' he was breaking her heart of course but no more than he was determined to break his own, occasionally he fired his pistols into the air in front of our building which brought down the odd sparrow, pigeon or lost gull, 'And none shall pass,' he whispered to the dead birds as he buried them, 'none shall pass,' he would surely have been institutionalized had he not taken a fall up or down the stairs of our building one afternoon, the doctor diagnosed some cracked ribs and a floating kidney, 'Here's the thing,' he told our maid, 'let him neither cough nor burp nor hiccup nor fart nor laugh,' in other words my father definitely out of action for an indefinite time, something of a blow to him for sure, 'But much, so much remains to be done,' he moaned which was about the only thing still permitted him as he rested, our maid read him tales from 'The Thousand and One Nights' and or paraded nude in front of his bed to either calm or excite him, whichever would come first, 'Cuddle up a little closer,' my father sang which our maid took for a definite sign of improvement, she gently stroked his cracked ribs and pressed softly on his kidney to keep it from floating, in the fading light she created shadow puppets on the wall to remind my father of happier days gone by, 'Truly tremendous.' my father whispered, she placed his unloaded pistols under his pillow for support, 'Better,' my father sighed, 'yes, much better,' she made him lentil soup with bacon fat, 'Ah, the sure way to a man's heart,' my father sighed, meaning his stomach of course, and soon, soon he was as good as new or ever or only slightly worse, he entered the city's Pioneer Day Marathon where he was the oldest runner by far, the mayor presented him with a medal for his remarkable last place finish, 'They also win who strive and finish last,' the mayor intoned as part of his unbearably long and meandering speech, my father smiled and coughed up blood which by then was permitted him, the medal with its inscription 'Better Luck Next Time' depicted a griffin with a coiled snake in its beak, which reminded my father of one of his many coats of arms from centuries gone by, he threw the medal into the air and caught it between his teeth like the well trained dog he had become.

'Memory a curious thing,' my father told me. 'It can take you back but not forwards, in other words it both aids and retards the passage of time.'

By then my father given to pronouncements even he himself didn't fully understand.

He fell from the balcony of our fourth story apartment but landed on the pavement like a cat on its feet, he brushed himself off and rushed back upstairs to try again, this time purposefully tempting fate unlike the last.

In other words my father no believer in accidents.

'Everything that happens happens for a reason,' he lectured, 'but the reason unknowable, just as everything that happens happens within time with time itself a mystery of course.'

He broke out in frequent sweats which he matter-of-factly wiped with the back of his hand.

'Sweating words,' he smiled as our maid nodded.

'We nearly always believe we're on to something tremendous,' he continued, 'it's how we continue, carry on from one day, one decade, one century to the next, the tremendous has us by the balls, the gonads, it gives life and breath to nearly everything we do while squeezing us lifeless, breathless at the same time, we pursue it instinctively without letting reason interfere, obstruct in any way, along with reason we throw any and all caution to the winds, unknown to ourselves we are seeking death in life and life in death, we are never truly satisfied but want more and more of the same or something so different that we cannot possibly imagine it, what do you think kept me alive all those decades, centuries, eons if not the pursuit of something that forever eluded me, ending it all no solution, for ending just another way of seeking, in the end we leave nothing but dim traces of ourselves in the past, nothing solid or even half-way remarkable, our footprints in time barely distinguishable from all others, quitting not an option, or quitting just another of our countless options that surround and choke us to death, here's the thing,' my father finished, 'in the end we're damned whether we do or don't, seize or let go, damned or saved, it makes absolutely no difference, so, please,' he sheepishly looked at our maid, 'another bottle of wine if you don't mind,' and still sober or already drunk he headed for our balcony once more to yet again pit himself against fate, time, gravity and whatever else he might encounter, or to once more test his powers of flight and or plummeting without any natural or unnatural aids, in other words my father still the scientist poet or poet scientist he had always been, our maid quickly called the fire department to inform them of my father's repeatedly precarious activity, they came with a trampoline the size of a football field, and it was on this springboard that my father landed, bounced, landed then bounced again until he finally cleared our building and disappeared into the spring, summer, fall or winter clouds above.

'A good time had by all, don't you think?' he smiled at our maid on his return.

At which our maid wiped her hands on her apron as if wishing to have no more to do with him.

'Will you come away with me?' my father asked.

A question which had everything to do with my father but nothing with our maid.

As she fully realized. Or didn't.

My father painting verbal pictures of all the places he meant to take her.

Real as well as imaginary.

'Picture you upon my knee,' he sang.

By which he meant mountains, rivers, valleys, oceans, the works. Cities that glittered in the night same as the day. Night into day into night in other words.

'Lovers are very special people,' my father sang. Pulling our all the stops in other words.

Our maid listened and nodded.

'It's the same old song,' she replied.

Her voice quite a bit higher and a lot softer than my father's. My father not easily dissuaded.

If he didn't succeed at once, which he rarely did, he tried and tried again.

'There's a kind of hush,' he sang. And.

It was true.

Except for a mild breeze the night calm and peaceful for once, one, that is our maid, could easily imagine traveling endlessly in just about any direction, in other words starting from a single, a specific point and in time and with time winding up everywhere or nowhere at all, 'Are we there yet?' she would ask and they would be or not without it making the least bit of difference, and, here is the interesting and or important thing, with no traces of them, that is our maid and my father, left behind for anyone else to follow, in other words once gone they would be gone forever, beyond all boundaries including time itself, and, 'Tell me more,' our maid said although she didn't believe a single thing, not a single word my father was telling her.

'Neither time nor place a factor,' my father continued.

'Yes,' she nodded.

'And,' my father continued, 'neither you nor I a factor.' 'Yes,' our maid nodded.

And.

'Easy come, easy go,' my father smiled. 'Yes,' our maid smiled back.

'And we would come as well as go,' my father smiled, 'entirely disappear.'

And our maid smiled back.

My father reached for our maid. The pleasure of her company.

He thought he was entitled, had earned it by then.

I mean the smile, that smile still on her face as well as his. But.

'Not so fast, Charlie,' she pushed him away. And.

Back.

To square one.

Or two or three or four at the most.

My father as far as our maid was concerned.

'Ah, to melt your cold, cold heart,' my father sighed Which it really wasn't. Her heart that is.

No matter. But.

'To melt your cold, cold heart,' my father sighed.

I mean with everything else melting all around, and by this I'm not excluding the polar ice caps, why not our maid's heart, I mean was or wasn't it unreasonable that of all the things unmelted it should be our maid's heart to upset my father the most, in other words the ending of time the same as the beginning, or my father destined to die of a broken heart just as he had been born with one, he steadied himself in front of our maid then, pulled himself to his full height with his chest out and shoulders back, and, 'I will love you till the day I die,' he announced in a rather matter-of- fact tone, to which, 'The sun will come up tomorrow,' our maid replied, meaning it was too soon yet to talk of the ending of time but already too late to consider its beginning, and, 'How about a nice chocolate malt or a slice of watermelon or a glass of wine spritzer?' she asked, and bear in mind this was in the middle of winter or summer or spring or fall, neither of them sure by then, and, 'Sure,' my father replied, 'sure, a slice of watermelon would be just the thing,' and off they went in search of a watermelon, in or out of season, they had no idea.

My father ancient by then.
Nearly timeless by then or as old as time itself. And.
Our maid the same.
In other words he could recall, although at times more clearly than others, his days as star dust, an amoeba, a reptile, a tree shrew, a baboon and so on and so forth, our maid the same, and he could still recall his first longings, yearnings in those various stages, our maid the same, which only increased, multiplied with the passage of time, 'Time is longing itself,' he once announced to just about anyone who would listen, in other words, 'As we are creatures of time,' he told our maid, 'let's just love within time until time itself shall end,' our maid with different ideas, in other words love timeless as far as she was concerned, and, if she had ever loved my father, which she had of course, she loved him beyond the boundaries of time which at times confused the hell out of my father, just about, 'Seize the day,' he often pleaded with her, or the night, the hour, the minute, the moment, no matter, but his love and hers in and of different dimensions it seemed, perhaps it had been different at the beginning or would be near the end, no way of telling, but neither my father nor our maid quite sure just how to handle something as evanescent yet all-important as love let's just say, in other words my father pleaded and our maid refused, a pattern repeated over decades, centuries, eons of time, with my father often feeling he was stuck in no man's land and our maid in no woman's, no matter, or, 'Will

you just gaze into my eyes?' my father begged, to which, 'Just look at that sunset,' our maid replied, in other words the more things changed the more they remained the same as far as my father was concerned, although not in all things and all ways, and, 'When will you be mine?' my father finally asked, to which, 'When the rivers run dry, the cows come home, when time will end,' she replied although not without the hint of a smile which my father could interpret any way he liked depending on his mood and or circumstances, 'Ah, but we could make such beautiful music together,' he sighed and took out his violin or viola da gamba, at which point our maid ran to her room or the hills, whichever seemed closer at the time.

'Call me Frankie,' Pizarro told my father.

My father with no great love for the man, even less than he had for Columbus and his haughty ways, still he tagged along, that is my father, for the love of adventure and or the proverbial gold at the end of the rainbow, 'Here, take this mosquito repellent,' Pizarro handed him some ointment made from the bark of the gumbo limbo tree, no sooner had Pizarro landed in the so-called New World than he considered himself an expert in all things great and small, my father put the ointment in his bag, he never used it, Pizarro in his ridiculous suit of armor struck him, that is my father, as strangely out of place as well as touch, his bearded, elongated face struck him, that is my father, as nothing so much as a goat's in heat, and what did my father care for the founding of new cities, Lima for example, when there were already so many, too many in other parts of the world, I mean what was Lima to my father and my father to Lima, my father bedded some native women of course, but never, I repeat, never did he let them take him for some sort of a god, I mean fair is fair, unlike the so-called Conquistadores my father more than willing to learn a number of the native songs as well as teach quite a few of his own, in fact, 'What sort of a man or men go around calling themselves Conquistadores?' he often asked himself, uncouth and unmusical on the whole, born killers he soon enough realized, every last one of them, in the business of claiming not land so much as death for Spain, in fact, 'Inglorious bastards,' he, that is my father, often whispered under his breath, the last straw was the entrapment and murder of Atahualpa, the Inca chief himself, 'Tell me you're not going through with this,' my father pleaded with Pizarro, to no avail, in Atahualpa, 'Call me Ata,' the Inca chief had told him, that is my father, but in Atahualpa my father had always found a man willing and eager to listen, to learn, although with that stubborn native streak of course, it goes without saying, my father often presented him, that is Atahualpa, with various mathematical puzzles that the chief found both amusing as well as challenging, for example, 'If train A travels at sixty miles per hour towards point X,' my father said with a gleam in his eyes, 'and passes train B at three thirty in the afternoon traveling at sixty miles per hour towards point Y in the opposite direction, what color are the eyes of the engineer driving train A?' brain teasers for sure, and, bear in mind, this was well before the invention of the locomotive, but the chief had an infectious laugh, no matter, but, as I said, the killing of Ata the last straw as far as my father was concerned and after Pizarro's own assassination by a rival Spaniard, 'Good riddance to bad rubbish,' my father mumbled, he, that is my father, escaped into the jungles with some of his favorite native women in tow, wound up and settled in Cuzco for a spell where he sired and pretended to raise any number of sun children as he called them, but in the end the climate, the jungles, the natives, the Spaniards and even his own children got the better of him, and, "Adio, Casablanca,' he said and returned back home to our maid who for a time did her best to please him, that is my father, by preparing certain Inca dishes my father was forever raving about, that is before she got fed up with the sight, smell and taste of them all and returned to making stuffed cabbage, fish soup and beef goulash.

At any rate the ingredients for the Inca dishes nearly impossible to obtain.

'Does this mean you don't love me?' my father asked. Our maid nodded in the affirmative.

'You bet your sweet Andes it does,' she answered. To which my father had no reply.

He simply lowered and shook his head.

And.

'Jeepers, creepers,' my father sang or said to our maid. 'What?' she asked.

And.

'Where'd you get them peepers?' my father sang or asked. 'What?' she asked.

And.

'Where'd you get those eyes?' my father elaborated.

And my father would have continued of course, I mean the best lines still to come, but our maid fed up by then, sick and tired of my father's so- called singing, I mean my father no Frank Sinatra or Frankie Lane or even Frankie Avalon as far as our maid was concerned.

She would have settled for Rudy Vallee I think. I mean even he would have been more bearable. So.

As there was a revolution going on, one of many of course, my father decided to throw himself into the melee, in other words to become a revolutionary without quite being one, in other words unarmed, unprepared and dressed in nothing but his sports jacket and khaki pants my father headed for the streets, and, 'Don't you start or finish without me, boys!' he yelled at the top of his voice, I mean he could be heard not just for blocks but for miles around, and the killing spree already begun, I mean in earnest not just in fun, and it was boys against men and men against soldiers and soldiers against tanks, in other words the battle or battles uneven as sooner or later most battles are, and need I remind you that without a weapon of his or anyone else's choice my father the perfect target, moving, weaving, bopping of course but still the perfect target, nevertheless in the midst of all the madness my father still with the boldness if not entire presence of mind to sing out, 'We're a long way from Tipperary!' or Titicaca he could have substituted to nearly the same effect, but the point was my father was both where he did and didn't want to be, in other words witnessing both what he did and didn't want to witness, and it had been this way for decades, for centuries, for eons of time, lacking any convictions of his own my father swept up and along by the warring convictions of everyone else around, and with bullets whizzing and shells exploding all about, my father both did and didn't feel himself to be in his elements, impossible to say, and stepping, skipping, jumping over the wounded, dying and already dead my father thought, 'Are we done yet?' a rhetorical question if ever there was one, and it wasn't until he began seeing our maid's face in those of the wounded, dying and already dead, in other words substituting our maid for the wounded, dying and already dead that he thought he had better get the hell out of there, in other words revolutions would come and go but not so our maid, I mean that was his thinking at the time, in other words to lose a revolution or two was certainly annoying but to lose our maid nothing short of a tragedy, I mean that was my father's thinking at the time, so he made a bee or beaver or mole's line back to our building, and it's just too bad my father wasn't Dorothy in another piece of fiction and so could have just clicked his heels and gotten there in no time, but Dorothy Dorothy and my father my father of course, he arrived tattered after hours, days, perhaps even weeks of not fighting as well as fighting, of not shooting but being shot at in other words, our maid quickly bandaged his visible as well as invisible wounds, and, 'This is what you get for meddling in madness,' our maid chided, to which, 'This is what I get for loving you to madness,' my father replied, in other words once again our maid focusing on one thing and my father on another, but at this particular time or on this particular occasion all was well that ended well, which it didn't or wasn't of course, no matter, in time and with time my father made a satisfactory if not entirely full recovery, and for months, for years afterwards he would display his scars to whoever was willing to see, with some words of explanation to confuse and or mislead the unwary, 'The wounds of love,' he would tell them, at which our maid just smiled and shook her head before heading off to the market to buy some live chickens and or carp to feed the guests that piled into our apartment.

My father a page turner for Beethoven.

'Call me Wiggie,' the great composer told him. That is my father.

Beethoven with a sincere liking for my father in whom he saw the ridiculous and so the entertaining personified, in other words my father terrific for taking Beethoven's mind off other matters, in fact about the only thing that annoyed the maestro about him, that is my father, was that wild hair even more explosive than his own, that is Beethoven's, 'Can't you do something about that mass or mess,' he often regarded him, that is my father, no matter, talk was that my father was about the only one with whom Beethoven got along in a manner of speaking, Beethoven no pussycat to put it mildly, but no doubt my father under the spell of his passion, that is Beethoven's, in other words his music, 'But where does this come from?' my father asked about a certain melody, theme or movement and Beethoven immediately pointed to his heart, in other words entirely bypassing his head, or, 'Yes!' Beethoven shouted, 'It's the eternal yes of life!' in time and with time my father getting used to Beethoven's shouts, as a matter of fact his music that is Beethoven's, nothing but the shouts from his broken heart according to my father, and, as my father's own heart had already been broken into a million pieces by then he, that is my father, could well understand as well as appreciate, but Beethoven the master, the champion of broken hearts as he, that is my father, clearly realized, he, that is my father, put up with a lot of crap because of it, at times he, that is Beethoven, treated my father like the lowest of servants while at others like a trusted fellow sufferer, my father carried Beethoven's luggage as well as his scores on the maestro's gigs through European capitals, 'What's keeping you?' Beethoven often shouted from a waiting carriage, but let's just say that those times were some of the most hectic as well as beautiful in my father's long life, Beethoven's, 'It has to be!' rang in my father's ears, his, that is Beethoven's musical shouts and shouted music took my father for spins in as well as outside himself, that is my father, in other words I think it's fair to say that in their various travels, in the time spent in each other's company my father didn't know whether he was coming or going, or now coming, now going depending on the master's moods, in other words the inside the out and the outside the in as far as my father was concerned in Beethoven's company, and this spell, since that's what it was, only broken at a recital in Stuttgart or Leipzig, Beethoven nearly or completely deaf by then, in other words already composing and playing music he, that is Beethoven, heard one way and his listeners another, in other words Beethoven nearly or completely isolated by then, no matter, but it was at a recital in Leipzig or Stuttgart that my father suddenly imagined or saw, in other words recollected our maid's face, and this while listening to this isolated man's recital, but my father didn't know whether the music had birthed our maid's face or the other way around, he rushed back home to find out, and with Beethoven's music still ringing in his ears he, that is my father, embraced our maid and lifted her clear off the ground, and, 'You are the music!' he shouted, and for once our maid didn't struggle, not at first at any rate, sensed the madness in my father's words and arms, and it was only after the madness abated that she dared collect herself, and, 'Put me down you big ape,' she finally whispered, whispering most effective she must have figured, and my father unhesitatingly obliged, in other words my father finding it impossible by then to handle both our maid and Beethoven's music at the same time.

And.

My father growing or grown tired of everything about himself, I mean given his incredibly long life sooner or later it was bound to happen, or, 'Is this all there is?' he asked our maid on more than one occasion, in response to which she served him some cold borsht or sour cherry soup, but my father suddenly recalled his times with Kepler and Brahe, 'Ah, the good or bad old days,' he mused, I mean in those days people were still burnt at the stake for a lot less than what Kepler and Brahe and my father saw or claimed they had seen, and my father with a longing for the days, the times when people were burnt for the sake of an idea or ideas, not that he wished such a death for himself but in some ways perhaps he wouldn't have minded, and, 'It's all out there,' he gestured one starry night to our maid who merely complained of the unseasonable chill in the weather, no matter, but he made up his mind to begin gazing at the heavens once more, he even quoted one of his favorite poets to our maid, 'All of us sitting in the gutter but some of us are staring at the stars,' he told her while she was trying to figure out whether the cold wind was out of the north or the west, no matter, but my father decided to turn the hunting lodge on one of his abandoned estates into an observatory, a few simple additions like that of a tower would more than suffice, 'Think, just think what we will see with modern instruments,' he grabbed our maid by the arm, to which, 'Watch the pronoun,' she replied, meaning he would be on his own as far as any star gazing would be concerned, she packed him sufficient provisions for his journey into the countryside though, 'Keep them in a cool, dry place,' she even told him about the sausages, not that it mattered, and warned him about the local builders who would rob him blind before they would be done with his tower, to which, 'They're not dealing with an infant, a neophyte,' my ancient father replied, and in the end she had to let him go of course, in some ways my father worse than Beethoven once he got an idée fixe into his head or worse than Icarus once he decided to get ever closer to the sun.

'Don't wait up for me,' my father told our maid on departing.

And.

'It'll be something or nothing,' he added.

It was weeks or months before my father took up his residence in the tower, in other words weeks or months before he first turned his instruments toward an as yet uncharted and perhaps even unseen dark part of the universe, and, my father expecting nothing did certainly get something for his efforts, in other words countless bangs for his bucks, the births and deaths of stars, or matter annihilated by antimatter or the other way around, the hints, quite definite, of black holes, of dark mass and energy, 'Ah, now I'm cooking with gas,' he even kidded himself, but in the end he got no nearer his ultimate quest of catching a glimpse of the beginning as well as the ending of time, in other words in his tower in the woods he was as close or as far from his goal as he had been in the bedroom of his apartment, in other words as they were both constituted of time the great mystery of the universe no greater than the mystery of human life with time still beyond his grasp, he had his tower torn down and his expensive instruments sold to a second-hand dealer on Váci Street, 'Slightly used is still used,' the dealer successfully argued, and to our maid's nagging query as to what he had seen, discovered and learned he merely shook his head and shrugged, finally he told our maid point blank, 'Let me tell you, I would give the entire Milky Way for a glimpse of one of your milky white breasts,' at which our maid nearly blushed, I say nearly because by then she was quite used to my father's exaggerations.

In fact, 'A sigh is just a sigh and a tit just a tit,' she even smiled. Which my father appreciated of course.

In lieu of what he was truly after.

'Now tell me about black holes,' our maid prompted.

But my father's notion of black holes and our maid's entirely different by then.

An accidental meeting.

As so many of my father's meetings had been throughout his interminably long life.

In other words on Vienna's Kärtnerstrasse he bumped into Freud or Freud into him, no matter, but the analyst looking down and my father up, in other words neither of them seeing where they were going, 'A thousand pardons,' Freud instantly remarked, to which, 'No, no, the fault is all mine,' my father responded, Freud bent down to pick up his glasses then straightened and scrutinized my father, and, 'An interesting type,' he, that is Freud, mumbled, that is my father struck him as something of a civilized savage, in other words a creature of both civilization and its discontents, and, himself a great lover of them, 'Where did you get that dashing hat?' Freud inquired, to make small talk no doubt, my father named a place on Landstrasse-Hauptstrasse, 'Ah, indeed, indeed,' the analyst nodded, nothing impressed him more than the right hat on the right head, and, 'Can I tempt you to an espresso?' he, that is Freud asked, with his total disbelief in accidents Freud guessed, figured or even realized that meeting my father was not without some underlying purpose, 'There must be something deep there, he even mumbled to himself, in other words having met my father he wasn't about to let him go just like that, not without some digging into the hidden layers of my father's mind that is, and, 'I know a lovely place,' he took my father's arm, 'all the spent Russian exiles and would-be revolutionaries gather there, he was thinking of Trotsky among others of course, although this had absolutely nothing to do with either him or my father, no matter, and, 'Play your cards right,' Freud winked at my father, 'and I may even treat you to one of their excellent strudels,' and, it must be admitted, by this time my father was beginning to enjoy himself, something about the man's, that is Freud's, intensity fascinated him, that is my father, so arm-in-arm they headed for the Café Central with its elegant glitter, Freud's very words, 'Don't you just love this elegant glitter,' he asked my father on entering, 'the lovely façade, the fabulous pretense?' Freud with a way with words of course which my father soon enough realized, more of a poet really than a so-called scientist, 'Please, please, make yourself comfortable,' Freud pointed to a table, a chair by the window, and, 'A window to the soul,' he even gestured as he admired the view outside, and, 'Zwei Schwarze,' he held up two fingers for the waiter who immediately bowed and disappeared, 'Now, how about you and I get acquainted?' Freud smiled, by which he meant he, that is Freud, very much wanted to get

acquainted with my father but not the other way around, which, again, my father soon enough realized, and, 'You strike me as the timeless type,' he, that is Freud, leaned close, 'but, of course, it's the timeless types who are the biggest captives of time itself,' my father let it go, he didn't mind, because if there was any thing he loved to discuss with just about anyone it was the various dimensions and or effects of time, 'And of course time is nothing more than our wishes, desires, our drives,' Freud continued, 'in other words our sexual urges,' Freud winked at him, that is my father, with which my father both agreed and disagreed, in other words while my father's sexual drives were at least as strong as Freud's, although not as twisted perhaps, he, that is my father, realized, in fact knew that there was a lot more to time than the mere push to copulate, so, so, 'Now wait, just a minute,' he objected, but by then Freud off and running, and once he got going there was no stopping him, not even by my father, and, 'We are the playthings of the gods, of our passions,' Freud continued, and, my father feeling a little uneasy at this simplistic formulation, this reductionism signaled for the waiter and the promised Freudian strudel, and, 'So how do you explain a Leonardo, a Michelangelo, an Einstein?' he, that is my father, asked, and as he had personally known them, he, that is my father, nearly called these great figures by their pet names, in other words Lenny and Boni and Al, which Freud, not being the timeless man my father was, wouldn't have understood of course, and, 'Sheer, pure sublimation,' Freud replied, which didn't exactly sit well with my father, in other words it annoyed the crap out of him, 'But enough, enough of this,' Freud waved, 'just tell me a little bit about your childhood if you don't mind,' which my father considered of course, but over his interminably long life my father had had so many different childhoods that it would have been impossible to recall let alone recount them all, so, 'No,' my father replied, 'but how about discussing your lovely sister-in-law instead?' which of course was and always would be a sore point with the analyst, in other words don't ask, don't tell as far as his sister-in-law was concerned, the poet but not the scientist or the scientist but not the poet in him visibly upset, and, 'Just who is asking the questions here?' he, that is Freud, fixed my father in his gaze, to which, 'You mean just who is the analyzer and who the analyzed,' my father quite cleverly and or appropriately replied, my father with this notion formulated way back when during his prolonged stay in Hellenistic

Byzantium that the analyzer and the analyzed were one and the same, I mean for practical and or impractical purposes, in other words that for everyone, which included Freud and himself, the observer and the observed were one and the same, and at that time, meaning sitting in the Café Central with Freud, he, that is my father, was more than willing to elaborate on this notion of his which, if true, would have canceled any sort of need for a so- called outside analyst, in other words negated the much cherished and even essential role Freud envisaged for himself,

Freud perceptive, keen enough to realize this at once, and, 'Chilly,' he, that is Freud, simply remarked, 'don't you find it getting chilly in here?' and this, it must be noted, in the midst of a heat wave in late summer or early fall Vienna, no matter, and, 'Ah, where does time fly?' he, that is Freud, added for good measure while glancing at his engraved silver pocket watch, and he, that is Freud, politely but firmly excused himself, and, 'Hysterics wait for no one,' he smiled as he called for the bill, and, 'Please, please,' he glanced at my father, 'you stay, enjoy yourself, I'll have the Ober add a strudel to the bill,' and it was a piece of that very strudel, quite tasty if a bit on the sweet side, that my father wrapped up, pocketed and carried back home to our maid, 'And this, he said as he handed it to her, 'because no matter where or when or with whom I never stop thinking of you,' our maid took a bite and instantly made a face, and, 'Mine are lighter and more tart,' she confronted my father who had to agree of course, still, our maid polished it off then washed it down with Bull's Blood, and, 'Do you think I'm getting a bit too fleshy about the hips?' she asked, at which my father was ready to grasp to feel for himself, but our maid's just a question, not an invitation, and my father once more finding himself in deep or shallow waters depending on one's preference of metaphors.

'You take Chronos,' my father lamented over dinner one night, 'The Greek god of time.'

And.

Our maid groaned. How could she not? But.

'Chronos who only creates in order to consume his children,' my father continued.

And.

'How is the pudding?' our maid asked. And.

'Excellent,' my father had to reply.

But even with pudding in his mouth my father with Chronos on his mind, and he seemed to recall an etching, if that's what it was, of Goya's, 'Chronos Devouring His Children,' although he couldn't be sure, he had known Goya personally of course, 'Call me Frank,' stretched any number of his canvases, but Goya a bit on the morose side, and while his, that is Goya's, interest in time mirrored my father's or the other way around, he, that is Goya, coupled his with painted visions of the atrocities of the world, in other words as a master and or companion Goya getting on my father's nerves after awhile, still, pudding or no pudding, my father with Chronos on his mind.

And.

'A penny for your thoughts,' our maid smiled. But.

My father sensed a trap as well as the next man, in other words Chronos Shmonos as far as our maid was concerned, so he once more complimented her pudding, its color, texture but most of all its taste, and left or postponed his musings about man-eating gods for another time and place.

In fact, 'Time is not on our side,' he simply said.

That night our maid entered his dream and in the company of Chronos of all creatures, and from the very first image my father sensed some kind of close perhaps even intimate relationship between the two, across a desolate landscape, like Goya's perhaps, they, that is Chronos and our maid, approached my father hand-in-hand and with their mouths wide open, and about the only uncertainty in the dream was who would begin devouring him, in other words our maid or Chronos, or love or time, and perhaps in the end it would make no difference but in my father's mind, in other words in his dream it most certainly did, and he reached for her the way he had so often in his life and pleaded, begged, 'Please, please, let it be you,' and that's when he woke, in other words without ever discovering whether it would have been our maid or Chronos to have swallowed him in his dream.

He pounded on her door.

'Please, please, let it be you,' he begged.

Our maid a sound sleeper though, in other words nothing, not even my father's pounding could penetrate her dreams, in other words her dreams hers and my father's my father's and our maid never woke to open her door.

My father imploded.

Sooner or later it was bound to happen.

I mean in time and with time he was bound to implode, shrink and eventually disappear.

Finally.

Step out of time if you will. Our maid by his side.

Where else would she have been?

My father speechless and measureless by then.

In other words he had stopped speaking, measuring, calculating and in any way symbolizing by then, in other words what you saw, that is our maid saw, was what she got, finally, and of my father's once bulky, impressive frame, time with a lot to do with it of course, only his eyes remained the same size they had always been, and it was to be near, as close as possible to those eyes that our maid undressed and slipped beneath the blanket next to my father's ever shrinking figure, in other words time and the timeless finally collided then, or our maid still in time but my father fast leaving it, and in his eyes our maid glimpsed not only herself but everything of the past, present and the future as well, in other words following my father she too was ready to step out of time, and it was in this fashion, in other words lying side-by-side, that they were eventually discovered, two time-bound and now timeless creatures of whom only their eyes remained, in other words wide open even though they could no longer see, the attending physician saved them of course, why would he not, and to this day they lie preserved in separate glass boxes in the State Museum of Oddities, with everyone free to look, to examine, free admissions Saturdays and holidays.

Mislabeled of course.

His eyes for hers and hers for his. It goes without saying.